The Saturday Secret

Miriam Rinn

Illustrated by Spark

Alef Design Group

LIBRARY OF CONGRESS CATALOGING-IN-PUBLICATION DATA

Rinn, Miriam, 1946–

   The Saturday secret / Miriam Rinn

   p. cm.

   Summary: Frustrated and angry over his new stepfather's strictness about Jewish traditions, such as being kosher at home and observing the Shabbat, twelve-year-old Jason fights for the right to play baseball on Saturdays.

   ISBN 1-881283-26-7 (alk. paper)

   [1. Stepfathers—Fiction. 2. Jews—United States—Fiction. 3. Baseball—Fiction] I. Title.

   PZ7.R478Sat 1998

   [Fic]—dc21   98-22138

                                           CIP

                                           AC

ISBN# 1-881283-26-7

ALEF DESIGN GROUP • 4423 FRUITLAND AVENUE, LOS ANGELES, CA 90058

(800) 845–0662 • (323) 582-1200 • (323) 585–0327 FAX • WWW.ALEFDESIGN.COM

MANUFACTURED IN THE UNITED STATES OF AMERICA

Chapter 1

"So long, Wayne, see you tomorrow. I'll bring over my Ken Griffey rookie for you to look at. It's awesome."

"Later, man," Wayne said, holding his hand up for a companionable slap.

Jason Siegel watched as the tall, husky black boy moved toward the front door of the large Tudor-style house, then started ambling toward his own house two blocks away. The warm breeze ruffled the sunny forsythia shrubs that dotted almost every lawn in Shady Glen, New Jersey, in the April dusk. Baseball practice had run late, and then the two sixth graders had stopped to check out the newest X-Men comics. It had to be after six, Jason thought.

Suddenly, his heart began to beat faster. It was Friday, and his mother had warned him to come

1

home right after practice. He still had to shower and change before his grandparents arrived for Shabbat dinner.

Jason began to run, his backpack thumping with each step. His stepfather David would certainly be home and cleaned up by now, and his mother would have bathed his twin half sisters, Leah and Devorah, and dressed them up in their Shabbat clothes. Jason thought it was the stupidest waste of time and energy he'd ever seen. It was dumb to change clothes for a couple of hours, just to eat a meal. They were only going to hang around the house, the way they did every Shabbat, so why did it matter what he was wearing?

Jason stopped running when he reached his walk, slipped the backpack off his shoulders, and began fumbling in the outside pocket. Where was that *kippah*? David had asked him to wear it, but he always took it off as soon as he left the house. That was another dumb thing David wanted him to do, something he'd never even thought of before his mother remarried a little more than two years earlier.

Finding the skullcap, Jason grabbed his backpack and mitt with one hand and jammed the crocheted *kippah* onto his thick brown hair with the other. One of David's old ladies at the nursing home where he worked had made it, crocheting "Go, Mets" around the rim. Jason knew his stepfather had hoped that would make it more appealing, but Jason wasn't buying it. Just because David had discovered Religion with a capital *R* didn't mean Jason had to turn his life inside out. He scowled as he struggled to grab the doorknob. Let David boss his own kids around; Jason was tired of taking orders from him.

Jason pushed the door open and dropped his stuff on the floor. Stepping quietly into the hall, he glanced right. Sure enough, the dining room table was covered with a tablecloth and set for five, with two high chairs. The Shabbat candles on the sideboard were not lit yet. Maybe he could get into the bathroom before anyone saw him and there wouldn't be a problem.

"Jasee here! Jasee here!" a voice squealed gleefully, and Jason turned around to see Leah trying to follow him up the stairs. He sat down on a step, smiling despite his anxiety, and waited for the chubby twenty-month-old to reach him. Her white tights were already gray at the knees, and the red ribbon that should have been around her head was looped dangerously around her neck.

"Hey, cutie pie. How's my girl?" Jason hugged the little girl and rested his cheek on her silky blonde hair. He loved the twins much more than he'd expected when his mother got pregnant six months after she'd married David. They were the best part of his new family, he often thought. "Where's your partner in crime?" he asked.

4

"She's right here, all ready for Shabbat." David stood at the bottom of the stairs, his reddish beard neatly combed and his thinning beige hair covered by a *kippah*, holding an identical curly-haired smiling blonde in his arms. Jason gazed at Devorah's lightly freckled face, so much like her father's.

"We were wondering where you were," David said, looking up at Jason.

Jason flushed with irritation. "Practice ran late, but I'll go get changed now."

"Make it fast. Mom's about to light the candles."

Jason carefully balanced Leah on the stairs, snatching off the red ribbon and tossing it to David. "She's going to kill herself with this." Then he raced up the stairs to his room, ignoring her squawk of complaint.

As Jason stripped off his sweatpants and T-shirt and threw them toward his hamper, he glanced at the family photograph hanging over his bureau. It showed a woman with dark bushy hair laughing as a little boy tried to shovel snow. A man with long hair leaned on another snow shovel. Jason was about three years old in that picture, so it had to have been taken four years before his father died of leukemia.

Jason gazed at the picture, letting his eyes rest on his father's face, long and thin like his own. Whenever he thought of his father, he saw the face in the picture. It seemed to him that he remembered his father, but at times it was hard to know whether he remembered the man himself or stories and pictures of him. Jason often looked at albums from the time his father was healthy and strong, and when he didn't look at them for a long time, he felt that he'd done something wrong.

Jason stepped quickly in and out of the shower and hurried to put on slacks and a shirt. As he combed his hair, he thought he could hear his Grandpa Phil's voice downstairs. That meant they would be eating soon. Jason couldn't wait to tell his grandfather about practice and this year's team. Phil loved baseball as much as he did, and his candy store always sponsored one of Shady Glen's junior teams. When he was younger, Phil used to coach. Together, Jason and his grandfather worried about the New York Mets and whether that year's highly paid super-star would deliver.

"Grandpa, guess what?" Jason said, as soon as the whole family was seated around the table and David had finished blessing the wine and hallah. "I'm pitching this year, and Wayne is catching. We are going to be unbeatable. All the way with Jase for Ace!"

"And modest, too," Phil said, smiling, as he put an arm around his grandson's shoulders.

"Why should he be modest?" Grandma Estelle asked seriously. "Everyone knows he's a wonderful pitcher."

8

"It's okay, Mom," Shari Siegel reassured her mother. "Dad was just kidding Jason." She passed plates loaded with sliced pot roast, mushroom barley, and glazed carrots down the table, blithely ignoring Leah's hammering on her high chair with a spoon.

When everyone had been served and the girls had settled down to picking up slices of carrot, Phil said, "We have a birthday coming up, if I'm not mistaken. How about if all of us go into the city for Jason's twelfth. We can go to a show and then to Chinatown for dinner."

"Yeah! I'm going to use chopsticks for everything, even the fried rice." Jason bounced up and down in his chair from excitement. He loved Chinese food, and the weirdest and tastiest was to be found in New York's Chinatown.

His excitement was contagious, and shy Devorah began bouncing in her high chair too. David cleared his throat. "That's very generous, Phil, but that would cost a fortune."

"And it's so hard to find a sitter for the two of them," Shari quickly added. "I wanted to throw Jason a birthday party right here at home."

Jason sat very still. What was going on? Mrs. Rosario from next door would be glad to watch Leah and Devorah; she watched them all the time. His mother knew he loved Chinese food. They used to eat it every Sunday, but David couldn't find much that was kosher on the menu.

Jason watched as David shot his wife a grateful smile. That was it! David didn't want to go to Chinatown because it wasn't kosher enough, so Jason's birthday had to be ruined. It was too much for Jason to bear. "That's not fair," he cried out, jumping up and knocking his chair back. "You can't spoil my birthday," he yelled at David. "I'm sick and tired of all your stupid rules."

Jason ran out of the dining room, making sure to throw his *kippah* on the floor. He slammed the door of the family room shut and clicked on a video game. David had asked him not to play video games or watch TV on Shabbat, but he didn't care about that now. His stepfather's demands were never going to end, Jason was certain, until Jason's life was topsy-turvy.

"Knock, knock," Phil's voice called through the door.

"Who's there?" Jason asked automatically.

"Boo."

"Boo who?"

"Don't cry. It's only a joke."

"Ha, ha," Jason said, his eyes on the game. He didn't look over as his grandfather sat down on the couch.

"I know you're angry at David," Phil began.

"That's right, I am," Jason interrupted, thumbs punching furiously. "He's trying to mess up my life. Why do we always have to do what he wants? And why does Mommy always stick up for him? She's never on my side, never. Everything was fine before he showed up, and now everything stinks."

His grandfather gave a deep sigh. "Jason, you're still a boy, but you know that's not true. Your mother went through a very hard time after your father died. It's not easy to lose a husband and be a parent all alone. It broke my heart to see her so sad. When she met David at that high school reunion, she started to come back to life. I thank God for him. He may be a little serious," Phil continued, "but he's good for your mother, and I know he likes you. He's never been mean to you, has he?"

"I guess not, but this religion thing is driving me crazy. He never asked me if I wanted to be observant! First, we have to be kosher at home, so no cheeseburgers or bacon. Then I can't have tacos in school or pepperoni on my pizza. Now, no TV or Nintendo on Saturday. I might as well go to bed when I come home from school on Friday and stay there until Saturday night."

Jason threw down the game controller in disgust. "That's it. I'm dead. You know what he did last Saturday? He wouldn't drive me to the library, and my social studies report was due on Monday! I would have got an F if Mommy didn't take me."

Phil looked at him closely. "How long did you have to do this report? Why did you have to wait until Saturday."

"I just forgot," Jason mumbled, "but that's not the point."

"So what is the point?" Phil asked, standing up. "He wants you to do stuff that he thinks is important, and you don't. And you want him to do stuff that you think is important. I think both of you need to consider the other guy's point of view and give your mother some peace. God knows she deserves it."

Phil held his hand out to Jason and pulled him up. "Let's go back and see what's for dessert. Your mother was always a great cook, kosher or not. God knows where she learned, because Bubby can just about boil a cup of tea."

Jason giggled in spite of himself. "That's why you like to eat out so much."

"You got it, sonny. I know every diner from here to Hoboken."

When Jason and Phil got back to the dining room, Shari was just cutting up a large chocolate layer cake. "Just in time," she said, glancing up and smiling. "David reminded me there's a new kosher Chinese restaurant over in Mayfair, Dad. Why don't we go there for Jason's birthday? We'll bring the girls, and Jase, you can invite some of your friends. Doesn't that sound like fun?"

Jason looked at his stepfather, who smiled at him. "I guess. Do they have lo mein?"

"Never heard of a Chinese restaurant worthy of the name that didn't," David answered. "We'll have a good time, and it's not as big a shlep."

Jason looked at his mother, who nodded encouragingly. "All right," he finally said, swallowing the sour taste at the back of his throat. David had won again.

Chapter 2

Jason stared out his classroom window at the budding trees, tired of the consequences of Reconstruction. His social studies teacher's droning voice reminded him of the sound of cicadas in the summertime. The noise just went on and on, stopping momentarily, then picking up again.

"Jase," a different voice hissed nearby. Jason looked at Michelle Appelbaum from the corner of his eye and casually dropped his hand to grab the note she was holding out to him. Michelle was all right for a girl. She was smart and funny, and she played first base for Ace Hardware. Unlike the only other girl in the league, Michelle took baseball seriously. She wasn't playing just to meet boys, Jason knew.

Jason opened the note under his desk and looked down to read. Yes, he nodded to Michelle, he was going to Ashley McDonnell's birthday party. He wasn't going to miss his first boy-girl party at a nearby video arcade. The class had been discussing nothing else for the past two days.

"I'll take that, Jason."

"What?' Feeling suddenly hot, Jason looked up at Mr. Hayworth standing next to his desk, his hand out.

"You know what, and if you pass any more notes, you'll be taking one home to your parents. I've spoken to you about this before, Jason."

Jason handed over the note, flushing deeply. He would just die if Mr. Hayworth sent a letter to his mother. She had warned him that sooner or later his constant talking and joking would get him into trouble. He couldn't seem to help himself, though. Sometimes, the teachers were so boring, and he just loved to see his friends laugh at something he'd said. Michelle had told him that he was definitely the funniest kid in the whole sixth grade.

"I'm sorry, Jason," Michelle said later as they walked to science. "I didn't see him coming. He's such an old dirtbag."

"Hayworth isn't worth hay," Jason quipped, smiling in spite of himself at Michelle's peal of laughter. "Forget him. Don't we have practice today?"

"Yeah, at four-thirty. I wonder what Corsello comes up with today." Michelle shook her head, and her dark red hair went flying. "According to him, I can't do anything right."

Jason wound up and threw the ball straight into Wayne's glove. As it whizzed past the batter standing between them, the boy looked perplexed. He hadn't had time even to swing.

"All right!" Coach Corsello yelled from the dugout. "If you keep pitching like that, we're going all the way, Jason. Just keep your mind on what you're doing and don't goof off. The rest of you guys better wake up too."

The team huddled around the coach as he passed out game schedules. "We have two more weeks of practice. Remember what I told you at orientation. There are three things in your life for the rest of the season—Ace baseball, winning, and me. I'll see you on Thursday."

Jason and Wayne grabbed their caps and sweat-shirts and started to walk home. "Corsello's kind of rough, isn't he?" Jason said. "He gave Michelle a hard time when she missed that grounder."

"Jeff Reed said he was the worst coach he ever had," Wayne said. "He screamed at him right in the middle of a game when he walked two batters in a row."

Jason grunted, then changed the subject. "How are you getting to Ashley's party? Do you need a ride or something?"

"I'm not going."

Jason looked at Wayne in astonishment. "You're not? How come? She's giving everyone five bucks worth of tokens, I heard. It's going to be awesome."

"She didn't invite me, that's how come," Wayne said in a quiet voice. "It's no big deal. I can go to a video arcade anytime I want, you know."

"Yeah, I know," Jason reassured his friend, but he felt confused. Why wouldn't Ashley invite Wayne, one of the most popular kids in the class? He was an A student, a good athlete, and one of the few boys who could dance the way they did on music videos. It couldn't be because he was black. Ashley had always invited Shaniqua Williams to her birthday parties in third and fourth grade before Shaniqua moved, and she was black.

"See you tomorrow, Wayne," Jason called over his shoulder as they passed Wayne's house. "I'll call you later for the math homework."

"I'm home," Jason announced, opening the front door with one hand and clapping on his *kippah* with the other. "What's for dinner?"

"Don't yell," his mother called from the kitchen. "Come in here and you'll see."

Jason threw his sweatshirt on the stairs and headed into the kitchen. His mother, dressed in a stained green sweatsuit with "If Mama Ain't Happy, Ain't Nobody Happy" on the front, was trimming string beans. "What's for dinner?" Jason repeated, rummaging through the pantry for something to eat in the meantime.

"Lamb chops and baked potatoes."

Baked potatoes without butter or sour cream, of course, Jason thought crossly. "Gross. What else?"

"That's it. Of course, there's always bread and water."

"You're a riot, Mom. Here's my schedule for baseball. Our first game is against Larry's Cleaners. They're pretty good. And guess what? Ashley didn't invite Wayne to her party. Isn't that weird?"

"Does Larry's still sponsor a team?" David asked, walking into the kitchen with a bag of potato chips. "I played for them, believe it or not."

Shari Siegel began to laugh. "When did you play baseball? You spent most of your time getting people to sign petitions, as I remember." She gave her husband's cheek an affectionate pat. "Playing games was much too frivolous for a do-gooder like you."

"That was in high school, Shari. I wasn't born trying to save the world. It was a talent I developed as I went along," David objected, blushing slightly. "I was lousy at baseball so I had to figure out a different way to get next to the cute girls."

"Uh huh." Shari glanced at the schedule on the counter in front of her. "What day of the week are these games? There are just dates here."

David offered Jason the bag of chips. "Give it to me. I'll check the calendar while the girls are watching TV. Mr. Rogers will be over soon, and we'll be back in bedlam."

Jason grabbed the bag and began to cram potato chips into his mouth while David studied the calendar. "I can't believe she didn't invite him," Jason mumbled. "Why do you think she didn't?"

"Some of these games fall on Saturday," David said, "but you can play in all the others."

"What do you mean, all the others? I'm playing in all of them. I'm the pitcher."

"I don't think that will work out, Jason. Not only should you not be competing on Shabbat, but on Saturday morning you'll be in *shul* with the rest of us."

"*Shul!* Are you kidding? Since when do we have to go to synagogue on Saturdays?"

"Your mom and I talked about it, and we decided since the girls aren't napping in the morning anymore, we can go as a family. You'll enjoy it, Jason. A lot of the kids from your Hebrew school class are there, and you can hang out with them."

"I will not enjoy it!" Jason slammed his fist down on the counter in pure frustration. "And you don't care whether I do or not. You just want everything your way. Mom," Jason wailed, "tell him he can't do this."

Shari put her hand over her eyes and took a deep breath. "David, why don't you check on the girls? It's too quiet in there." When her husband left, she pulled Jason toward her and tried to hug his stiff body. "Can't you give him a break, Jason? He's trying to make us feel like one family. I know baseball is important—"

24

"It's the most important thing there is, and I'm going to play, whether he likes it or not! He can't tell me what to do!"

"Jason, please, I can't take this anymore! It's not going to kill you to go along with David once in a while. You're always fighting with him over nothing. Anyway, it's only three or four games." His mother's voice cracked as she pulled him even closer. "Don't we all deserve some peace and happiness after what we've been through? This is our chance. David wants you to love him, I know he does, but Judaism is so important to him. He gets all involved in things. He always did. Please, Jason, for me, don't turn this into a battleground."

Jason broke out of his mother's grip and raced upstairs to his room. His heart was pounding, and he felt as if he couldn't catch his breath. Anger filled his entire body, and he clenched his teeth to keep from screaming. His mother had sided with David again, just as she always did. Why wasn't what he wanted important to her anymore? Why was it always David, David, David? There was no way David was going to stop him from playing, he decided. No way. He'd be on that mound for every game, no matter what. He'd be on that mound for every game, no matter what.

Chapter 3

"It's over, thank goodness," Corsello called out. "Come on in."

Jason wiped the sweat off his upper lip and walked slowly toward the bench where the coach sat scowling. Jason knew what was coming. The team had played miserably during the practice game, and it was the last one before the regular season began. The final score was 12 to 2.

When the outfielders had loped over, Corsello began. "There's only one player here who has a reason to play like a girl. What's the rest of your excuses?" No one said anything, and the silence seemed to stretch out forever. Jason could dimly hear the other team laughing in the background. "If you want to beat Larry's on Saturday, play like you mean it, not like this… this joke that I watched today! You guys looked pitiful."

Jason stole a look at Michelle. She was chewing on her bottom lip and blinking her eyes rapidly. Although Corsello had gone on a rampage against everyone as the score widened, he seemed to single her out. The more he yelled at her, the more mistakes she made. She'd missed a tag at first base, then made a couple of other errors in the outfield, where he'd sent her. On top of that, she'd struck out two of her three times at bat. Jason knew she was a better player than that, but Corsello's constant criticism seemed to be rattling her.

"Miss Appelbaum," Corsello sneered, "I hope actually catching some balls on Saturday won't ruin your manicure. The rest of you, be here a half hour before the game starts; that's two-thirty. I don't want any last minute calls that you have to go to the ortho-dontist, or it's your great-aunt's birthday, or any of that baloney. Just be here, and be ready to play."

Michelle bolted as soon as Corsello stopped talking, and although Jason called to her, she ran straight to her mother's waiting car without turning around. Jason watched as Mrs. Appelbaum gathered Michelle into her arms; then he quickly looked away, feeling embarrassed.

After helping to put away the equipment, Jason picked up his mitt and fell into step next to Wayne.

"Wow, that guy is mean. Did you hear what he said to Michelle?" Wayne asked.

"You mean when she just watched that ball sail over her head?"

"Yeah. 'What are you doing out there? Planning what to serve at your next slumber party?' That's cold."

Jason was silent. Corsello hadn't bothered him much, but he could imagine what the coach would say if he told him he couldn't play on Saturdays. Jason shuddered involuntarily, remembering Michelle sobbing in her mother's arms. Being on Corsello's bad side was no fun, he was sure.

"I'll give you this hot rookie for your Nolan Ryan," Jason pleaded later that afternoon, sprawled out on Wayne's bed. Baseball cards covered the bed and half the floor of the third-floor bedroom. Both of Wayne's parents were working at Dr. Duggins' dental practice in the Bronx, so the boys had the large house to themselves.

"You want that old man?" Wayne scoffed gently. He knew Ryan was Jason's favorite player, and he enjoyed teasing him. "I'll give him to you, but I want that Dodger rookie too." Although he'd lived his whole life in New Jersey, Wayne was a Los Angeles Dodgers fan, to Jason's astonishment. He said it was a Duggins family tradition, from when his father lived in Brooklyn.

"You can have both of them. I don't care about the Dodgers."

"All right!"

"Wayne, I'm going to be in big trouble soon," Jason said suddenly, putting his new cards in his loose-leaf binder.

"Why? Did you forget to wear your little cap?" Wayne guffawed at his own joke.

"That's not it. David doesn't want me to play on Saturdays because it's the Sabbath and stuff, but if I don't show up for the first game, Corsello will burn my butt. I don't care what David says anyway, I want to play, but I don't know how to get there in my uniform and stuff."

Wayne became silent and thoughtful. "You're going to play even though your father doesn't want you to?" he asked after a minute.

"He's not my father! Stop calling him that." Jason slapped the binder shut. "He can't tell me what I can and can't do. I just don't want to get my mom all upset, so I don't want them to know."

"So how you going to sneak out of the house with your mitt and all?"

"Well, I thought I could bring it over here tomorrow, and then I could just come over and change right before the game."

"I guess you could. My folks wouldn't notice. They hardly ever come up here."

"If you were going to Ashley's party, I could tell my mom we were going together, and she wouldn't worry about where I was. She and David usually go out after Shabbat is over, so I could bring my stuff back in without them seeing."

"I'm not going, so that won't work. You need another plan, man."

It was Jason's turn to be quiet. "Are you mad she didn't invite you? I don't understand how come."

Wayne stared at his oversize basketball sneakers, then jumped off his bed and shot an air ball at an imaginary hoop. "I was upset at first. I just wanted to be asked, you know. But my old man wouldn't let me go anyway. He thinks I should have more black friends, and he was always telling my sister he doesn't believe in interracial dating before she went to college. I bet that was why Ashley didn't invite me."

"Why? Because your father doesn't want you to go out with white girls? She doesn't even know your father."

"No, you dope. Because there are no more black girls in the class since Shaniqua moved. Ashley was probably all worried about who I'd dance with. She should have remembered that you guys can't dance at all!"

Although Wayne laughed, Jason thought he looked unhappy. "Are you mad at your dad?" he asked impulsively. "That's sort of prejudiced, isn't it, telling you that you shouldn't have white friends. What business is it of his who your friends are?" It seemed as unreasonable to Jason as David's insistence that he eat different foods than all his friends did.

Wayne was silent for a moment. "I thought that at first, but I think he's just trying to protect me, keep me from getting my feelings hurt, you know. I'm not sure, but he always says that no one understands you as well as one of your own. He doesn't mean you, though. He's thinking about girls mostly."

Jason began to gather up his cards. He'd always been a little afraid of Dr. Duggins, who rarely smiled or spoke to him. Mrs. Duggins was always nice, though, friendly and touchy-feely. Jason suddenly recalled how she'd taken him around her house when he was little and told him about all the pictures on the wall. There were many of them, just as dark and serious as Dr. Duggins. Some were rel-

atives—grandfathers and great-aunts and such—
and some were famous African-Americans. He
knew they were famous only because Mrs. Duggins
told him. He'd never heard of most of them. That
was when he was in preschool and his father was so
sick. Jason was afraid of a lot of weird things then,
and portraits were one of them.

Jason was glad to learn that his friendship with
Wayne was in no immediate danger, but still, he
was taken aback by what Wayne had said. Dr.
Duggins obviously felt that he could tell Wayne
what he should do and who he should do it with.
Where did fathers and stepfathers get the idea they
could run their kids' lives? Jason wondered.

Chapter 4

Jason waved goodbye to his friends outside the synagogue and ran to catch up with the rest of the family. Saturday morning services hadn't been as bad as he'd expected. Leah and Devorah had gotten restless after about twenty minutes in the sanctuary, so his mother had asked him to take them out to the lobby. He'd spent most of the morning goofing off with his Hebrew school pals, once he'd handed the twins over to a bunch of cooing girls. The worst part of the morning was wearing a shirt and tie.

"Hey, wait up," he called, running down the sidewalk and pulling off his tie at the same time. David and his mother had already crossed the street with the stroller and were heading toward home. "What's for lunch?"

"There's turkey left over from last night, and kugel, and salad," his mother answered. "There should be apple cake, too, if David didn't polish it off last night."

David blushed slightly, saying sheepishly, "Well, there wasn't all that much left."

"I'll have turkey," Jason announced, then asked casually, "What are you guys doing this afternoon?"

"This afternoon?" David asked in a surprised tone. "What we usually do, I guess. The girls need to nap, and Mom and I could use the rest too. That's what's so great about Shabbat. No chores, no phone calls, no noise. Just perfect peace."

"Why, what are you doing?" Shari asked, looking sharply at her son.

"Aah, I don't know," Jason answered. "I thought I'd go see Grandpa down at the store after I change. You know," he added, smiling broadly at David, "pay him a Shabbat visit. We need to talk about those Mets."

David laughed. "That sounds fine, Jason. Phil will be glad to see you."

Jason looked back at his mother, who smiled and gave his hand a squeeze. It was working so far. Shari and David wouldn't expect him back till dinnertime, and the game would have ended long before that.

Lunch over, Jason poured himself another glass of ginger ale and glanced quickly at the clock above the refrigerator. "I guess I'll go down to the store now," he said, lifting the glass to his lips.

"Okay." David carefully arranged the lunch plates in the dishwasher. "Wish your grandfather a good *Shabbes,* and have fun. Tell Phil I don't mind if he gives you a ride home, as long as Shabbat is over."

"Oh, wow, thanks!" Jason said over David's chuckle and pulled the door shut behind him.

As soon as he got out of sight of his house, Jason stuffed his *kippah* in his pants pocket and began to run. It was already a quarter to two, and he and

Wayne had to be at the field at two-thirty. Thank goodness Wayne's house was on the way to his grandfather's candy store. Otherwise, he would have lost time doubling back.

Panting, he burst into the foyer as soon as Wayne, already in uniform, opened the door. "Come on. It's late!"

"What took you so long?" Wayne compiained. "You said you'd be here by 1:30."

"I couldn't just race out. I had to make it look like I wasn't in a hurry."

"Your uniform is in my room, where you left it, and your mitt's up there, too. Hurry up. Corsello will bust a gut if we're late."

By the time Jason reached Wayne's third-floor bedroom, he could hardly breathe. Quickly, he pulled off his sneakers and stripped off his shirt and jeans. He fumbled in the bag for his cup, put it on, and then put on the rest of his uniform. "I'm coming," Jason yelled in response to Wayne's demands that he hurry. "I have to find my batting glove. Here it is."

Jason ran down the stairs, wondering briefly where Wayne's parents were, then remembering they kept the office open for a half day on Saturdays. "All right, all right, let's go!"

"You should have left your bike at my house. Then we could have rode," Wayne said, jogging beside Jason.

"My mother keeps the stroller in the garage. She would have noticed." His side was beginning to hurt. "Let's slow down. We'll get there in time. This is killing me."

Wayne and Jason arrived at the field just as Corsello pulled up in his pickup truck. "Okay, boys, are you ready to play?" the coach called out as he gathered up the equipment.

"We're ready," Jason said, slowing down so he wouldn't overtake Corsello.

"You better be. Let's ace it for Ace." Corsello walked away toward the bench, laughing at his own joke.

Jason looked at Wayne and shook his head in disbelief.

The first pitcher for Ace was Chris Logan, a seventh grader. Jason watched from his position at third base as Chris began to pitch. The first two pitches were too high, but the third was a strike. Chris was a reliable pitcher once he warmed up, so Jason wasn't worried. The team they were facing didn't have that many good hitters.

"Strike!" The first batter was out, and the second came up to the plate. He hit a wobbly ball toward first, which Michelle quickly scooped up, and then Chris struck out the third batter.

"Hey, hey, hey! Great beginning, team. Now let's get some hits." Corsello pulled at the brim of his cap and studied the batting order. "Duggins, then Giuliano, then Lindenbaum. Get us going, Wayne."

41

Jason sat down on the bench next to Michelle, and together they watched Wayne take his stance at the plate. He held the bat high, shuffled his feet moving a bit away from the plate, and looked toward the pitcher. The first pitch came in, slow and straight. Wayne swung smoothly, and Jason heard the crack as the bat connected. Flinging the bat down, Wayne began to run toward first base. The ball sailed over the infield and bounced in center field. As the outfielder ran to pick it up, Corsello began to shout, "Go to second!" Wayne kept running and arrived at second base just before the ball did.

A cheer went up from the Ace bench. "Did you see that awesome hit? He could have made it to third, I bet," Michelle said.

"Wayne's not that fast, but he can sure hit."

By the end of the third inning, Ace was comfortably ahead, and Corsello was all smiles. Jason looked at his watch. It was ten minutes to four. He had plenty of time to get home before dusk.

At the bottom of the fourth, the score was 12 to 2, with Ace in the lead. The team was ecstatic, and Corsello couldn't stop beaming. Chris Logan had pitched dependably, but it was clear that he was tiring.

At the end of the inning, Corsello announced, "You did fine, Logan. We're killing them. Let's give some of the other kids a chance. Miss Appelbaum"—Corsello tipped his hat toward her—"you pitch this next inning. Logan, go to first."

When Jason glanced at Michelle, she looked ghostlike. "Don't worry, Michelle, we're ahead by ten runs. Nothing can happen," he whispered.

"I hope not. He'll kill me if I mess up," she said, grabbing her mitt, and loped to the mound.

Michelle wound up and threw the first pitch. The batter hesitated and swung a moment too late. Strike, the umpire signaled. Jason could see

Michelle exhale in relief. The next two pitches were balls, however, and the following seemed to be guided directly to the bat. The batter made it to first before the ball was caught.

"Don't worry about it, Michelle. You can do it," a voice rang out from the stands. Jason glanced over to see Mrs. Appelbaum making a thumbs-up motion to her daughter.

If Michelle had heard her mother cheering, she didn't show it. She seemed focused entirely on the plate. She threw two strikes in a row, followed by two balls, and then another strike. "Way to go!" Mrs. Appelbaum screamed.

Jason glanced at his watch. Four-fifteen. The next batter was Joey Lipton, a brawny seventh grader. He was known as a slugger. Corsello started waving to the outfielders. "Back up, back up!"

Michelle looked scared. "Hang in there, Michelle. You can take him," Jason called out.

She looked down at the ground, wound up, and then threw a ball right into the dirt at the batter's feet.

"What are you doing?" Corsello shouted. "Don't you know where the strike zone is?"

Michelle pulled her cap down, then pitched another ball that sailed over the batter's head. "Don't worry, Michelle. Just relax and throw the ball," came from the stands. Jason saw Mrs. Appelbaum glaring at the bench where Corsello sat scowling.

After another two balls, Lipton walked to first, and the other hitter advanced to second.

When Jason looked at his watch again, it was quarter to five and still the top of the fifth. Michelle had walked the last three batters, giving Larry's Cleaners two more runs. The score was now 12 to 4, and Coach Corsello was visibly irritated. Jason was getting tired of standing on third base, and he looked worriedly at the lowering sun. How long was it till dusk? It would be dark by six o'clock or so, and he was sure his mother would call his grandfather as soon as Shabbat was over to find out what they were doing. If Michelle kept walking batters, the game would go on forever. Their league had no limit on the number of walks, and there was another inning to go after this one.

Suddenly, Jason heard the crack of the bat and saw the batter race toward first. The second baseman snagged the fly, tagged the runner heading toward him, and got the ball to first in time. Finally, it was time to head back to the bench.

"Are you running a pitching clinic on what not to do, Miss Appelbaum?" Corsello raged in the dugout. "What's your plan? Keep Larry's here until they give up from exhaustion?"

As Michelle hung her head, Jason spoke up, "Coach, why don't you put me in next inning? I can finish this game in a hurry, and then we can all go home."

Michelle's head jerked up, and she glared at him in reproach. "Thanks pal," she whispered. "I needed that." Without another word, she turned and went to the far end of the bench.

"Okay, Siegel, you're in, but now get over there and put on your helmet. You're up after Jordan."

Jordan was tagged at first, Jason singled, but the next two batters struck out. It was as if everyone wanted the game to end quickly. He checked his watch as he walked to the mound. Five-twenty. The sun was sinking into the horizon behind him, and it was difficult for Jason to see Wayne's mitt clearly. He squinted and concentrated on getting the ball across the plate. There was no time for mistakes. If he couldn't strike three batters out quickly, his mother would surely find out he hadn't spent the afternoon with his grandfather. Jason had never told his mother a lie this big, and he couldn't imagine what she'd say to him.

"Strike!"

Jason wound up and threw again. He knew it would be a strike before it reached Dwayne's glove, the ball was moving so fast. One more, and this guy was history.

The next batter was gone in minutes, and the third almost as fast. When Jason ran over to the dugout, Corsello slapped him on the back. "Great job, Siegel. I should've put you in right away, instead of our little miss here."

Jason didn't look at Michelle. "Uh, thanks, but I got to leave right away, Coach, before we clean up and stuff. Wayne and me have to be somewhere really important, and we're late already."

Corsello blinked at him. "Okay, I guess, but don't do this again. Call one of the other guys for practice times."

"Come on, Wayne, let's get out of here!" Jason called, and the two boys began to run in the twilight.

Chapter 5

Jason quietly opened the door and stood silently in the foyer, trying to catch his breath. The tangy aroma of spices filled the air, and he could hear David's deep voice singing the prayer that marked the end of the Sabbath. Even though Jason had made it home from Wayne's in time, he felt strangely filled with dread. What if they found out? What would David do?

Jason could see the family gathered around the tall braided Havdalah candle. Its flickering flame illuminated their faces. David held the tiny cup filled with spices close to Devorah's nose. The blonde head jerked away. "Stinky, stinky!"

"Hi, Jase, did you have fun with Grandpa?" Shari asked as he stepped into the kitchen.

"Jasee here, Jasee here," Leah squealed, running over and grabbing his leg. He picked her up, and she promptly tried to push a half-eaten cookie into his mouth.

"No, Leah! You can have it, okay?" Jason pushed his sister's sticky hand away from his mouth and avoided looking at his mother.

"Okay," Leah agreed cheerfully, struggling to get down.

"So what did you and Grandpa do all afternoon?" Shari persisted. "Eat candy bars and talk about the Mets?"

Jason slowly bent over to deposit Leah on the floor, keeping his back to his mother. "Oh, the usual, you know. We just talked, and stuff."

"Give the kid a break, Shari," David interrupted, putting his arm around Jason. "He doesn't have to give us a full report."

Jason suddenly felt deeply tired, as if he'd run a marathon. "I'm going to go upstairs for a while. I have to take a shower before Ashley's party anyway."

Shari looked at him in exaggerated surprise. "You? Jason Siegel is going to take a shower without his mother nagging him? Call CNN, Dave, this is a breaking story."

Jason didn't turn around but headed toward the stairs.

"Jase, are you all right?" his mother called out after him. "You look worn out."

"Yeah, I'm fine, but don't make me anything to eat. I'll eat at the party." Jason slowly climbed the stairs and closed the door of his bedroom behind him. Kicking off his sneakers, he threw himself on his bed facedown. His plan had worked. Shari and David believed he'd spent Shabbat with his grandfather. Why did he feel so lousy?

Jason turned his head and stared at the photograph of his father. The bearded man seemed to be looking right at him. Jason squinted so that the face became fuzzy and then opened his eyes again. His father's familiar face slowly came into focus. Why did he have to die? Jason asked himself for the thousandth time and fell asleep.

"Jason, what are you doing in there? I thought you were going to a party."

"Huh?" Jason opened his eyes to darkness. It took a moment for him to recognize his own room. "I guess I fell asleep. Wait, I'm getting up."

Light streamed in from the hall when his mother opened the door. "Dave and I are leaving for the movies soon, so if you want a ride, you better hustle." She hesitated, peering into the room. "Jason, I know how disappointed you were not to play today, and I want to thank you for—"

"Uh, that's okay, Mom. I have to get dressed now, all right?"

"All right. We'll see you downstairs. I hear Mrs. Rosario at the door now."

Jason sat on the edge of the bed and tried to will himself into a good mood. He'd only done what David had forced him to do, after all. He'd really had no choice. His father never would have forbidden him to play baseball on Saturdays or any other day. His father had loved sports, just as Jason did. Jason felt a sudden painful pang of loneliness. Why was he the only one who remembered his father? His mother never seemed to think of him at all, she was so wrapped up in David and the twins.

Jason shook his head and tried to focus his thoughts. What should he wear to Ashley's party? Maybe the jogging suit he'd received for Hanukkah. Yeah, and his Tampa Bay Buccaneers cap. He didn't care much about the Buccaneers, but he liked their colors.

"Pretty sharp," David said when Jason came down the stairs. "The girls should be impressed."

"I don't care about any girls," Jason retorted, blushing. "I'm only going because we get to play as many games as we want."

David smiled. "We'll swing by and pick you up after the movie. That should be close to ten o'clock."

Jason had the back door of the station wagon open before David came to a complete stop in front of the arcade. "Bye," he called out, slamming the door behind him. He didn't want his mother to get the idea she should walk in with him. Standing just inside the door, Jason scanned the room for familiar faces. He could see Michelle standing next to a couple of kids playing Deathblow and Ashley, wearing patterned leggings and a long sweater in the same color, handing out tokens to her guests.

"Happy birthday, Ashley." Jason handed her a wrapped package. "You're going to love this present. My mother bought it."

"Cool." Ashley dropped a pile of tokens into his open hand. "I heard about the game, Jason. You were really awesome, but what happened to Michelle? Did she, like, fall apart or something?"

"She just had a bad day, that's all. The coach really rides her. It wasn't such a big deal." Jason was puzzled. How did Ashley hear about the game? The only sport she played was shopping. Maybe one of the other kids had told her.

"Hey, Michelle, what's up? Are you going to get to play soon?" Jason peered at the current player's score. Deathblow was his favorite arcade game since his mother and David had lectured him about its brutality.

Michelle turned her back to him and stared at the game silently.

"Michelle, did you hear me? Are you next? Let's play two-man."

When Michelle turned toward him, her eyes were glittering with tears. "You've got some nerve, you creep, talking to me! Isn't it enough that you humiliated me in front of the whole team? I thought you were my friend, but you're not! You're just a low-life kiss-up. Don't you ever talk to me again. I hate you!"

Jason stood frozen in horror as Michele stalked off to join a group of girls at the snack bar. For a minute, he felt the curious looks of the other boys waiting to play; then they turned back to watch figures being decapitated and disemboweled. What was Michelle talking about? How could she say those things to him after he'd helped end the game?

Certain that everyone had heard Michelle yelling, Jason looked desperately at the clock. It was only five after eight, fifteen minutes after he'd arrived. "Jason, come over here," a voice called out. It was Mike Lindenbaum. "This is the greatest game. I already have the third highest score ever. I have the Nintendo version at home, that's why," he added as Jason quickly moved to his side. "Some game this afternoon, huh?" Mike chattered on as his thumbs jabbed buttons. "I thought it was going on forever. Good thing Corsello took Michelle out."

"Yeah, I guess. Say, do you think Michelle was upset that the coach sent me in to relieve her?"

Mike glanced at him. "Probably. Nobody likes to be called off the mound. And your volunteering didn't make her look too great. But she was pitching lousy. What did she expect? Look, this is where I jump three levels at once."

Jason watched the screen, but his mind wandered back to that afternoon's baseball game. He'd been so worried about the time he hadn't thought about Michelle at all.

He drifted about from game to game, carefully avoiding Michelle and her girlfriends, had a few slices of pizza with Mike and some of the other guys, watched as Ashley opened her gifts, and kept checking the clock. The party couldn't end fast enough for him.

At quarter to ten, Shari Siegel walked into the arcade, and Jason ran toward her. "Okay, Mom, let's get out of here."

"Wait a minute, did you thank Ashley and her mother?" Shari asked, blinking at all the lights.

"Yeah, yeah, let's go now."

"Okay, David's right outside."

As Jason and his mother opened the door, Mrs. Appelbaum stepped up, ready to come in. She shot Jason a look of pure hatred, ignored Shari's greeting, and pushed past them to enter the arcade. "What in the world…?" Shari murmured. "You'll never guess what happened," she said to David as she got into the car. "Lisa Appelbaum totally cut me! I've known her for ten years, and we've never said a cross word. I'm going to call her when I get home and find out what's going on."

Jason inhaled sharply. What was he going to do now?

Chapter 6

"Thanks, Louise," Jason's mother said, handing the short, plump woman some folded dollar bills. "David will walk you home."

"Oh, Shari, I should pay you, I love those little girls so much." As nervous as he was, Jason groaned inwardly. Mrs. Rosario said the same thing every time she babysat for Leah and Devorah. What if his mother agreed one night and held her hand out?

"Good night." David held the door for the babysitter and then followed her out.

Jason shuffled from foot to foot as his mother hung up her coat, his mind racing. He had to stop her from calling the Appelbaums. As Shari Siegel walked into the kitchen and reached for the telephone directory, he blurted, "You can't call now, Mom. It's so late. They'll all be asleep."

"They just got home from the party, Jason, like us. They won't be asleep yet. I want to know why Michelle's mother is angry at me. Did you see that look she gave us?"

"She was looking at me, Mom, not you. I'm the one she's mad at. You don't have to call her."

"You? Why is she mad at you? What did you do?"

Jason looked at the floor and pulled at the brim of his cap. "Well, it's about Michelle, it's, you know, about going out and stuff." He could hear the blood thundering in his ears as he stared at the blue-and-white tile on the kitchen floor.

"Going out! Why, Jason, do you like Michelle Appelbaum? I had no idea sixth graders were thinking about stuff like that. Well, I like Michelle, too. She's a nice kid, and pretty cute." Jason's heart began to slow down. He could hear the affectionate amusement in his mother's voice. She was so tickled that her "little guy" was growing up, she was forgetting about Lisa Appelbaum. "But, I don't understand something," Shari continued. "Why is Mrs. Appelbaum mad at you? Jason, did you do something to hurt Michelle?"

"Well, not exactly. It's more like a misunderstanding. Mom, please don't call. It's just going to make things worse. I promise I'll fix it tomorrow at Hebrew school. Really, it doesn't have anything to do with you."

"All right, Jase, but I don't want you to take this lightly. It's easy to hurt people without intending to, when it comes to romance."

"What does that mean?" Jason asked, following his mother upstairs and into the twins' darkened bedroom.

Shari leaned over each crib, lightly touching curls and smoothing the quilts that covered the sleeping girls. She turned and put her index finger up to her mouth, then walked down the lighted hallway into Jason's room, picking socks off the floor as she went and tossing them into the hamper. Sitting down on the bed, Shari smiled at him. "When boys and girls like each other in a special way, they become very sensitive. So you have to be sensitive to the way the other person feels." Her eyes moved to the photograph on the wall. "Daddy was a very romantic guy, too, so I guess I shouldn't be surprised at you."

Jason plopped down next to his mother. "Did girls like Daddy?" he asked, knowing the answer.

"Oh, Jason, I've told you a dozen times already."

"I want to hear it again."

Shari laughed. "Okay. They loved him, and he loved that they loved him. Your daddy had girls calling him all the time, and back in the dark ages, girls didn't do that often. He broke a lot of hearts, your dad."

"So why did they, call him, I mean?"

His mother looked at him in the semidarkness. "Because Daddy was so cute. He was tall and well built from all that tennis, and he was funny, and he could be so sweet. I had a crush on him from the first day I saw him in tenth grade."

Jason blurted, "Is David as romantic as Daddy?" He'd never asked that before.

Jason's mother's expression turned serious. His head was not much lower than her own, he noticed. "That's really none of your business, but I'll tell you anyway. David is a different sort of man than your father was, but he's one of the best men I know. We're lucky to have him."

"We'd be luckier if Daddy was still here." Jason bit his lip and looked at his shoes.

Shari put an arm around him and squeezed. "That's not what I meant, and you know it. We weren't lucky with that, for sure. But now we have another chance, a chance to be happy and to be a whole family again. David cares about us, Jason, really cares, and that's worth a lot."

Jason turned his head and buried it in his mother's neck. "I just don't want to forget about Daddy, and I don't want you to either."

Shari kissed Jason's hair. "Daddy will always be here, Jason. Nobody is forgetting about him. All I have to do is look at your face, and I think of him. And I'm sure somewhere he thinks about us too." She got up then and walked toward the door. "Nighty-night."

Jason sat on his bed, staring at the lighted doorway. He could hear David in the kitchen, opening and closing the refrigerator. So he cared about them, so what? His father had cared too, but that hadn't kept him well. Caring was no guarantee of anything.

Jason dawdled as he walked to the synagogue the next morning, not eager to run into Michelle before Hebrew school began. She'd probably yell at him or ignore him, as she'd done at Ashley's party. He didn't need any more of that.

He walked into the room just as Mrs. Horowitz was calling the class to order. "All right, boys and girls, let's pick up where we stopped on Wednesday. Did everyone read the chapter on Jews in the Ottoman Empire?" He slipped into his desk, and although he avoided looking toward the window where the girls sat, he knew Michelle was in her usual seat. What was he going to say to her? He felt his face get hot just at the thought. She hated him; she'd said so in front of everybody. If he didn't apologize, though, his mother would find out about the game. He just knew it. He had to talk to Michelle at the end of class.

"Uh, Michelle, wait a minute, okay?" Jason's voice sounded weak to his own ears.

"Are you talking to me?" She turned and stared at him, as the others noisily left the room to go to the next class.

"Yeah, I have to tell you something. I'm sorry about the game and everything. I didn't know you'd be so mad."

"Well, how did you think I'd feel?" Michelle asked in a low voice, looking at the floor.

"I don't know, I thought you'd be relieved, you know, because you weren't pitching so good and all. I thought you'd want it over with."

"I did want it over with, but not like that. You just made me look worse. And now Corsello has something else to pick on me for."

"I didn't think about that, Michelle. I was so worried that we wouldn't finish in time. I'm really sorry." A window opened in front of Jason's eyes. He could see the baseball diamond as it looked late yesterday afternoon. But now he was in Michelle's place on the mound, and his pitches were going all over the place. Suddenly, he felt ashamed. He'd told his mother a big lie, he'd hurt Michelle's feelings, and he'd tricked David. What was happening to him?

"Why were you worried about the time?" Michelle asked, looking up.

"If I tell you, you can't tell anyone. It's really important, okay?" Jason hadn't intended to tell Michelle about David, but suddenly he wanted her to know.

"I promise. You can trust me. I'll never tell." Michelle moved slightly closer and turned her head so her ear was near his mouth.

"My stepfather said I couldn't play ball on Saturdays, so I told him I was going to see my grandfather."

"So?"

"So, they would have called him as soon as Shabbat was over."

"Oh, you mean you were worried you wouldn't get home before dark."

"Yeah, and if you kept walking people..."

Michelle grimaced. "Don't remind me."

"It's so unfair that he won't let me play, just because he's religious. Why do I have to do what he tells me? He just wants me to hang out with them and die of boredom." Jason felt outrage bloom inside him, pushing aside the shame.

Michelle chewed the cuticle on her thumb thoughtfully. "Well, he probably thinks that the family being together on Saturday is more important than a ball game. What kinds of stuff do you usually do on Shabbat?"

"Just hang around. Sometimes my mom reads stories out loud, or we go visit people, or play with my sisters. Stuff like that."

"That sounds sort of neat. My family's too hyper to ever do quiet stuff together. Everyone always has a million places to go."

Jason stared at Michelle. "You've got to be kidding. You'd rather hang around the house than play baseball?"

Michelle's face clouded over. "I'm not exactly having a great time this year."

"That's just because Corsello's such a jerk. You're a good fielder, and you could pitch too if you practiced." Jason picked up his book bag as younger children began to enter the classroom. "We better go, but how about if I buy you some French fries at my grandpa's this afternoon and we figure out what to do about Corsello."

"Hey, Grandpa, I want to treat my friends to something good," Jason called out as he, Michelle, and Wayne clambered onto the stools that bordered the long black Formica-covered counter at Phil's Luncheonette. Grandpa Phil had been serving sandwiches, fries, and ice-cream sodas to the kids in Shady Glen for forty years. Jason still loved to look through all the new comic books and magazines in the rack at the back of the store, and Grandpa Phil had promised he'd let him work the register when he was fourteen.

"Okay, big spender, what will it be?" Grandpa wiped the counter off where they sat down and looked at them expectantly.

"I'll have an orange soda and some French fries, please," Michelle ordered.

"Give me fries too, and a hot chocolate, with lots of whipped cream," said Jason.

"Coming right up." Grandpa dumped some frozen potato sticks into the deep-fat fryer. "How about you, Wayne? What would you like?"

Wayne scanned all the food pictures and advertisements behind the counter thoughtfully. "Well, maybe I'll have a bacon cheeseburger, fries, a black-and-white milk shake, and a ginger ale."

Grandpa smiled while Michelle and Jason gaped. "You're on a low-fat diet, I see. Enjoy it now, sonny, because soon you'll be my age and eating cantaloupe cubes and water-packed tuna."

Jason heard the bell over the door jingle as his grandfather busied himself at the grill, and then Michelle groaned, "Oh, no, it's him!" When he looked to the side he saw Corsello standing at the register.

"Give me three quick-piks and a *Sunday Sentinel.*" Corsello paid for the lottery tickets and the newspaper without ever turning around and left the store.

Phil put the food in front of them. "Okay? The ketchup's over here. Enjoy. I'll be back in a minute."

Jason dunked a French fry into the hill of ketchup on his plate and chewed silently. Michelle and Wayne were eating just as quietly when Grandpa came back to lean on the counter. "What's wrong? The food not greasy enough?"

Michelle laughed. "No, it's perfect, Mr. Rothstein. It's just that our baseball coach was here, and we don't like him too much."

"Who, Charlie Corsello? He was a great ballplayer when he was a kid, but he was a sucker for an outside ball. He had a temper, too, I remember."

"He still has a bad temper, and he's taking it out on Michelle," Jason interrupted. "He picks on her all the time."

"He hates me and I don't know why," Michelle said, her voice cracking. "I've always been an okay player."

"What's your record?"

"We won our first game, only because Jason relieved me."

"Michelle has trouble making the ball go where she wants," Wayne explained tactfully.

"Maybe I could help you a little, if Jason and Wayne will field," Grandpa said. "I used to coach baseball when my kids were young."

"Grandpa's teams won championships four years in a row, and my uncle played baseball in college," Jason said, wiping ketchup off his shirt.

"Can you imagine, I offer my son the opportunity to stand on his feet seven days a week bending over a hot grill in this store, and he decides he'd rather go to law school?" Grandpa asked, his eyes twinkling.

"Who can figure out these kids nowadays, right, Grandpa?"

"Right, so why don't you help me close up, and we'll go out and throw a few."

Chapter 7

"Okay, Siegel, you get on third," Corsello barked. "You've pitched your three innings. Lindenbaum will take over. The rest of you go back to where you were."

Jason put on his cap and loped over to third. The score was 7 to 4 in Ace's favor. He'd pitched well, and Corsello was in a reasonably good mood. That could change at any time, though. Jason had seen in the last two weeks that his coach's mood depended entirely on the score. If Gilligan's Funeral Home got a few runs, Corsello would go nuts, as usual.

Jason focused on the play. The batter had just hit a grounder to the pitcher and was speeding toward first base. He was safe. Next up was Tyrone Lewis. Jason had been on his team the previous year and knew he was a slugger. Leaning forward and resting his hands on his knees, he prepared himself for whatever might happen. Jason could see from the swing of Tyrone's bat that the ball might go all the way. As he watched it arc and come toward him, he began to run backward, screaming, "It's mine!" He turned to run faster, still keeping the ball in sight. It was coming down now, and he was going to be there. Lunging forward, Jason held out his glove and felt the force of the ball jolt through his arm as it landed. Spinning, he waved back to the umpire. "I got it! I got it!"

Jason ran toward third, hurling the ball to Mike, who was staring at him in astonishment. He could hear the cheering from the bleachers and saw Wayne and Michelle dancing around in an embrace. Even Corsello was jumping up and down with excitement.

"Great play, Jason," rang out a familiar voice. "Way to go!"

Jason's head jerked around. He quickly scanned the bleachers. There, at the very top, were David and Grandpa Phil grinning at him and clasping their hands over their heads. A wave of delight washed over him. This was the first time David or Grandpa had come to a game, and he was glad they'd seen him make that catch. His mother had told him that it was too hard to run after the twins at the field, so she had not come to any of the games so far. Grandpa was usually in the store, and David came home too late, except for Tuesdays. This was the first Tuesday evening game they'd played.

He waved at his grandfather and David and turned back to the game. What was going on? Where was the kid on first? Jason heard the bat connect, but he couldn't see the ball. The batter was running to first and someone was running toward him. Where was the ball? Jason turned too late to see the ball coming toward him from the outfield.

By the time he ran to pick it up, Gilligan's had scored a run, and there was a player on third.

Shaking his head in disgust, he threw the ball to Mike and went back to his position. Glancing up at the bleachers, he saw David smiling sympathetically. His stepfather shrugged his shoulders in an exaggerated motion, as if to say, "What are you gonna do?"

"What the hell's going on with you, Siegel?" came a roar from the dugout. "Are you playing in this game, or another one on Mars?"

"Sorry, Coach, I got distracted," Jason murmured and turned around to see who was coming up to bat.

The inning finally over, Jason headed to the bench. The score was now 7 to 5, but they had two innings left to play. Anything could happen.

"Don't worry, Jason. You're still ahead. That was some catch." Jason turned around to see his stepfather leaning against the fence.

"Yeah, I can't believe I caught that." Jason walked over to David, then quickly put his hand on his head. "Uh, I have my *kippah* on under my cap," he lied.

David just smiled. "Your coach is quite a guy, isn't he? Really gets into the game."

"He stinks," Jason said, moving closer. "Just watch what he does if they get another run."

"Don't let him get to you. Some guys are like that. It has nothing to do with you." David gave Jason a thumbs-up sign and headed back to the bleachers. Jason watched as his stepfather climbed up to sit next to Grandpa Phil. The usual parents were there, including Dr. Duggins. He came to all the midweek evening games, except those that fell on Thursdays. He was a quiet observer, Jason reflected, never saying anything, even when Wayne did something terrific. Unlike Mrs. Appelbaum, who was always cheering and screaming and carrying on.

Jason inhaled sharply. Michelle's mother was only two rows below David and his grandfather. What if they started talking? Grandpa Phil had been coaching Michelle. Maybe her mother would want to say thanks or something. If she mentioned the game where he'd relieved Michelle, he'd be in it deep. Or what if David spoke with any of the other regulars? Anyone could tell him that Jason had been playing on Saturday.

"McMullen, Siegel, get ready," Corsello called out. Jason tried to shake away the apprehension he felt by swinging extra hard in the batter's box. He twisted his head from side to side and pulled on his batter's glove. He had to focus on the game now.

When Danny McMullen struck out, Jason stepped up to the plate. He adjusted his stance and looked directly at the pitcher. The first ball came toward him. He swung and missed. "Strike," the umpire called.

"Come on, Siegel. We need a hit," Corsello yelled.

"Choke up a little, Jason," came from the stands. Jason moved his hands up the bat. His grandfather had been urging him to do that for a while.

The ball looked big as it sped toward him. He swung from his shoulders until he felt the bat connect. As the ball sailed over the pitcher's head, Jason dropped his bat and began to race for first base. The ball had just bounced in near center field when he decided to go on. Sliding into second base, he heard the umpire call, "Safe!"

Michelle was next in the batting order. Jason watched her closely, looking for a chance to steal third. She missed the first two pitches, the next two were balls, and then she nicked the ball with her bat. It wasn't good enough to get her on first, but it was enough to get him to third. When the pitcher realized Jason was safe, he mouthed something in his direction. Jason laughed and turned to the bench to thank Michelle for getting him to third.

She was pulling off her batter's glove and looking for her mitt when Corsello said, "How about you let me do the thinking for this team, Miss Appelbaum, and you try to get a real hit."

At the bottom of the fifth, the score was still 7 to 5. A Gilligan's player was on second, and Corsello was pacing the dugout and picking fights with the referees. "He's only happy if we have a ten-run lead," Jason, who was in right field, grumbled to Michelle at first.

"What would make him really happy is if I disappeared."

"That was a smart play. It got me on third."

"Yeah," Michelle agreed. "We should have been able to bring you home. Uh oh, this kid can hit. You better move back."

Jason jogged backward and looked toward the plate. The first pitch was a strike. The batter hit the second pitch solidly toward first base. Keeping one foot planted on the base, Michelle leaned to her right to make the catch and then swiveled to throw the ball to third. Jason watched as the runner from second and the ball seemed to arrive at the same moment.

"Safe!"

"What! Are you nuts?" Corsello screamed. "Where did you park your Seeing Eye dog? He's out! You've got to be blind to call him safe!"

The field was silent except for the coach's shrieks and the murmur of the umpire. Jason watched Corsello's face get redder and redder until he finally stomped back to the Ace bench.

"Great play, Michelle! Way to go!" Mrs. Appelbaum cheered.

Michelle smiled when she heard Grandpa Phil call out, "That's playing smart." She waved at the stands, which brought a scowling Corsello onto the field.

"If you're finished taking bows over there, we have a game to win."

At the top of the sixth, Ace was ahead by only one run. Jason watched in despair as Mike Lindenbaum struck out, threw his bat down, and walked slowly back to the bench. He was gulping air, trying not to sob. "Stop blubbering, Lindabaum, or I'll throw you out of the game," Corsello raged. "You girls are playing like third graders, as if you never held a bat before. This isn't T-ball, you know. You're supposed to know how to play. What the hell do I have to do to get through to you? I don't have to be here. I could be home enjoying myself."

Then why don't you just go home and shut up? Jason wondered, as Corsello continued to pace up and down and yell at the team.

"Hey, what's going on here? Is this Little League or a major-league game?" Jason turned around to see David standing and staring at Corsello. His left

eye twitched, which Jason knew meant he was furious. "I thought I was here to watch my son play. How about we get back to the game and let these kids have some fun."

Corsello stood silently for a moment, his mouth open in surprise. Then he flushed a deep red, turned back to the bench, and said quietly, "Let's show them what we can do. McMullen, you're up next, then Siegel, then Michelle."

From the batter's cage, Jason peeked at David, who had sat down but was still frowning. Grandpa Phil was watching the field contentedly while the other parents chatted, sipped sodas, and called to little kids playing under the stands. Why hadn't any of them stood up to Corsello before? Jason wondered. Maybe they'd been afraid of embarrassing their children. Jason didn't feel embarrassed, he realized. He felt proud. David wasn't afraid of Corsello. The coach, like most bullies, had backed down when confronted.

The game finally ended in an 8 to 7 win for Ace. "You did okay, guys," Corsello said when they'd gathered in the dugout. "It was a squeaker, but we pulled it through. You know I get excited, but I don't mean nothing by it." He paused as the team stared at him in astonishment. "Anyway, I'll see you at practice on Thursday. We play C & C on Monday."

Jason glanced over, searching for David and his grandfather. They were standing by the refreshment stand, where Grandpa was wolfing down a hot dog, something he was forbidden to eat by Jason's health-conscious grandmother. Jason's grin faded when he saw Michelle's mother begin to gather up her things and climb down from the stands. He raced toward David, calling, "Let's go. I have a ton of homework, and I got to get started right away."

"Oh, Mr. Rothstein," Mrs. Appelbaum called out.

"C'mon, c'mon," Jason urged David, pulling him toward the van. "I'll never finish if we don't leave right now."

"Since when are you such a dedicated student?" David chuckled. "Okay, let's go. Phil, be well."

"Just don't tell Estelle about the hot dog." Grandpa Phil swallowed the last bite and turned to wait for Michelle and her mother.

Please, please don't let her tell about the Saturday game, Jason prayed as he climbed into the van.

Chapter 8

Jason frowned into the mirror, dissatisfied with what he saw. Something wasn't right. He squeezed more gel into his hand and rubbed it into his hair. Then he brushed the sides back vigorously. That was better. He looked cool in his new black shirt. If only he didn't have to wear his *kippah*. It would totally mess up his hair.

"Jason, are you ready yet? The girls are getting squirmy. What are you doing in there anyway?" his mother asked from outside the bathroom door.

"I'm playing strip poker. What else do people do in the bathroom?"

"Very funny," his mother replied as he opened the door. "Grandma and Grandpa are here, and we're all ready to go. Our reservation is for one o'clock, so I'm going to put the girls in their car seats. Make sure you turn the light off in your room, and turn off that radio. Now, where did I put those folding booster seats?"

His mother was in her military mode, as she usually was when they had to go somewhere. This Sunday afternoon they were headed to the new kosher Chinese restaurant in Mayfair to celebrate Jason's birthday. Michelle and Mike Lindenbaum were meeting them there, and Wayne's parents were going to drop him off a little later, after church.

When Shari Siegel bustled off, a huge bag of baby supplies hanging from her shoulder, Jason felt it was safe to wander downstairs. Phil hailed him from the living room. Putting his arm around Jason's shoulders, he said, "Here's the birthday boy. Happy birthday. We have some gifts for you, but leave them for later. It's already late. Estelle, why don't you ride with Shari and Dave in the van, and Jason and I will go together."

"Are you sure, Phil? Can you find the way alone?"

"Don't worry, we'll get there. Go ahead, Estelle. Sit in the back with the babies and keep them busy."

Satisfied that her husband wouldn't end up in Pennsylvania without her navigational skills, Jason's grandmother happily headed out the door to be of assistance to her daughter.

"So, what do you say we get going, Jason? We can have a little schmooze on the way." Jason felt his stomach clench as his grandfather looked at him. He didn't think this was going to be a how-about-those-Mets conversation.

Jason buckled his seat belt as his grandfather smoothly backed the big Buick out of the driveway. "Did you watch the Mets game last night, Grandpa? Did you see that homer in the fourth? That was unbelievable. I was so sure they were going to win—"

"Let's talk about another Saturday game, Jason. Mommy told Grandma that you weren't going to play baseball on Saturdays this year. So how is it

92

that Mrs. Appelbaum tells me you relieved Michelle?"

Jason slumped into his seat and scowled. "Why shouldn't I play on Saturdays? How come he can tell me what to do? I have to play, Grandpa. The team needs me."

Phil braked for a red light and looked over at Jason. "The team needs you, so you can lie to your parents? Where did you tell them you were going?"

Jason was silent.

"I didn't hear your answer. Tell me again," his grandfather repeated.

"To see you," Jason murmured.

"What was that?" Phil asked, catching up with the rest of the traffic. "You told Mommy you were going to see me? What if she'd called me? Did you think I was going to cover for you? You think I'm a liar, Jason?"

"No. I knew she wouldn't call you on Shabbat," Jason said softly. "That was why I wanted to relieve Michelle, so I could get home in time." Jason stared out the side window. His head was starting to hurt. "I couldn't think of anything else. It worked okay. They don't know." Jason turned around to look at his grandfather. "You don't have to tell them, do you, Grandpa? It's okay if they don't know."

"I don't think it's so okay, but I won't say anything to your mother. That's your job, Jason. Do you think it's right to lie to your parents?"

"I don't want to lie!" Jason yelled. "He's forcing me. He doesn't care what Corsello says, but I'm the one that's on his team. What am I supposed to do?" Surprised by his own outburst, Jason fell back against the seat. "I just don't see why playing on Saturday is such a big deal," he said more quietly. "You work in the store on Saturdays."

"Listen, my boy, there's an old Yiddish saying that every one makes his own *Shabbes*. What's good for me is not good for David. I don't have a problem with that, but I do have a problem with lying. That's not good for anybody."

Jason looked down at his new black-and-red basketball sneakers. His mother had given them to him for his birthday, saying he was lucky David was such a generous guy. Those sneakers could feed a family for a week, she'd added, just to rub it in.

By the time the Buick pulled into a parking spot in front of the restaurant, Jason's head was throbbing. He jumped out of the car, gulping fresh air, and looked around. Mayfair looked a lot like Shady Glen, except the downtown seemed larger and busier. When two boys around his size walked by, Jason noticed they both wore a *kippah* on their head.

"There you are," Shari called out from a few yards down the street. "How do you rate a spot right in front?"

Her father chuckled. "You have to be lucky and in the right place at the right time. The guy pulled out right in front of me. Where's the rest of the gang?"

"Mom and Dave are buckling the girls into the stroller. I was worried that the other kids were waiting in front of the restaurant."

"I think this is them, Mom. That looks like Mike's father's car."

Michelle and Mike scrambled out of the Cherokee that double-parked next to Phil's car. "Happy birthday, Jason." Michelle smiled and handed him a large wrapped box decorated with stickers.

"Yeah, happy birthday, Jase," Mike said. He held out a small brown paper bag. "You'll never guess what I got you. My father said it'll pay for college if you take care of it."

Jason shook out the contents of the bag and crowed with delight. "Awesome! Tom Seaver's rookie. Look at this, Grandpa. This has got to be worth five hundred bucks."

Phil examined the card carefully. "Well, it's a great card, that's for sure. I wish we had him for this season. Where'd you get this, Mike?"

"My uncle's getting married again, so he's getting rid of a lot of stuff. I figured Jase would want it even if one corner's a little bent."

"Thanks, Mike. This is great." Jason's headache had disappeared, and his spirits were lifting quickly. "Let's go inside. Wayne said he'd come in and look for us."

Jason, Michelle, and Mike walked into Moishe's Peking Palace and waited while David maneuvered the double stroller inside the door. "We have a reservation," Shari told the man at the cash register. "Siegel."

When the man checked his book, Jason noticed the skullcap on his head. "Party of ten, right? We're all ready for you. Do you want two booster seats?"

"These guys can reach the table on their own now," David said, draping his arms around Jason and Mike. Michelle laughed, but the man just looked confused, and David quickly added, "That's okay. We brought our own."

After parking the stroller in a corner, the Siegel party headed toward the back of the room. Three tables had been pushed together, Jason noticed, to make one long one. "Why don't you kids sit at one end," Shari instructed, "and Mom, you sit on one side of Leah, and Daddy will sit next to Devorah, and I'll be at this end—"

"Okay, Sergeant Shari," David said, taking his seat at the other end of the table. "We all have our assignments, so let's take a look at this menu. You guys can get whatever you want, and they have chopsticks here, too."

"Oh, I love chopsticks," Michelle said. "They're so cool. You can pick up one piece of rice at a time."

Jason looked around the restaurant while the others studied their menus. There were the familiar Chinese paintings of birds and mountains on the walls, and each table was equipped with the usual bowl of crispy noodles. The restaurant was about half filled with ordinary looking people. The only difference Jason could spot was that some of the men and women had forgotten to take off their hats.

"I think I'll get chicken fried rice and wonton soup. And a soda. Could I have an egg roll too?" Mike looked toward David.

"Sure. How about you, Jason? Have you decided?"

Jason looked at the menu carefully. There were beef, chicken, and fish selections and a vegetarian section. "I guess I'll have wonton soup, too." He raised his head to consult with Michelle, and his eyes fell on the front of the restaurant. Wayne was walking in the door. In his suit and tie, he looked like a tenth grader. Before Wayne could spot them, the man at the register leaped toward him. "Not today," he said, shaking his head. "You can come back tomorrow in the morning."

Wayne stared at the restaurant owner, confusion on his face. Jason felt baffled himself. Why didn't he just come back to where they were sitting? He raised his arm to wave but realized Wayne wasn't looking at him. He seemed struck dumb as the owner kept repeating he'd come at the wrong time.

People near the front were beginning to shift their attention from their food to what was happening at the door. "I think something's wrong." Jason pulled on David's shirtsleeve. "He won't let Wayne in."

David turned to see and immediately jumped up from his chair. "There you are, Wayne," he boomed across the room. "We've been waiting for you." He strode to the front and grabbed Wayne around the shoulders. "This young man is with us. Is there a problem?" he asked the owner.

"No, no, just a misunderstanding. I thought he was here to apply for a dishwasher's job. Here's another menu."

David grabbed the menu and steered Wayne to the table. "Why don't you sit right here, between Jason and me? Just move down one, Jase. Here's your menu. Now, have the rest of you decided what you want?"

"What happened, Wayne? Why didn't you come back here right away?" Michelle asked.

"I don't know. I guess I didn't see you." Wayne's dark face looked masklike, but his eyes glittered. He quickly looked down at his menu.

"I should have told the guy we were waiting for someone else. That was my fault, Wayne. I'm sorry you were embarrassed," David said softly.

"That's okay," Wayne whispered. "Stuff like that happens sometimes."

"It's shouldn't," David snapped. He took a deep breath, then he smiled. "All right, here's the waiter. Shari, you start down there."

As his mother ordered pineapple chunks for his sisters, Jason stole a sidelong look at Wayne. His friend looked sad and angry at the same time. Jason began to feel angry too. He knew there would have been no misunderstanding if Wayne were white. The unfairness shocked him deeply, and he was unprepared when the waiter got to him. "Uh, I guess I'll have moo shoo pork," he said, automatically ordering his favorite Chinese dish.

"No pork here. This is a kosher restaurant." The waiter bristled.

"How about moo shoo beef?" David interjected before Jason could begin complaining. When Jason nodded glumly, the waiter turned to Wayne.

"I'll have an egg roll, spareribs, pepper steak, and a ginger ale, please," Wayne ordered. "My sister is dating a Muslim guy, and he eats kosher food all the time, so I knew they wouldn't have pork or shrimp here. My spareribs are going to be beef, you'll see," he told Jason, loosening his tie.

"You're better prepared than most of us, Wayne," David said. "A lot of people don't know that the kosher laws forbid shellfish as well as pork. We should have invited your sister and her boyfriend to join us."

Wayne smiled. "They might have been a little late, Mr. Siegel. They're in college in Georgia."

"That's pretty far to come for a meal, all right," David agreed, laughing at Wayne's little joke. "But they can eat here if they come home for break."

"Only if we check the want ads first and make sure they're not hiring," Wayne answered, smiling at David's whoop of laughter.

Jason could tell his friend was beginning to feel better. Wayne was usually shy around grown-ups and rarely said anything to David, or even Shari, whom he'd known all his life.

The appetizers arrived then, and everyone was busy finding place on the table for all the platters and bowls of sweet sauce and hot mustard and rice. Wayne seemed to have forgotten about what happened, and Jason watched as his friends cheerfully struggled to pick up slippery egg rolls and wontons with their chopsticks. For an instant, he caught his stepfather's eye. David had struggled to make sure his birthday dinner was going to be fun, Jason knew, and he'd helped Wayne too. Gratitude washed over Jason as he realized how humiliated he would have been if David hadn't stepped in. It could have been a disaster, and Wayne would never speak to him again. David had done the right thing, just like he did with Corsello. How come his stepfather always knew what the right thing to do was with everyone else, Jason wondered, but not with him?

Chapter 9

The following Sunday afternoon, Jason was amusing himself by calculating the value of his card collection for the thousandth time when his mother came to the door of his room. "Are you going to be home this afternoon? David and I want to go out to do some shopping for a little while, and Mrs. Rosario can't come over."

Jason turned around from the cards he had spread all over his bed. "I was going to watch the Mets game with Wayne. He's coming over soon."

"How about if the two of you baby-sit Leah and Devorah? I'll pay you the going rate, and you can split it with Wayne. They don't have the patience to shop for more than twenty minutes."

"I wonder why, Mom." Jason returned to his cards. "Shopping is about as much fun as taking an English test."

"As an English teacher, I'm taking that personally," his mother cracked. Then she asked, "Do you think you can manage the girls all right? I'll give them lunch before we leave, and change them. All you have to do is play with them. If they get restless, read them a story. You know they always love that. Just keep an eye on them, and don't go outside."

"Yeah, yeah. Don't worry, Mom. There's two of us to two of them, and we're a lot bigger. Everything will be fine."

Wayne walked in just as Shari and David were leaving. "Hello, Wayne, I hope you like kids," Shari greeted him. "Jason, if you have any serious problem, call Grandma right away. She'll be home, but she has a cold, so don't bother her unless it's important. There's plenty of apple juice and yogurt and animal crackers, but don't let them eat any-thing if you're not there."

"Whatever. I've got it under control. Good-bye," Jason said, giving Shari a push out the door, as he held Leah with his other hand.

"Jason, make sure—" David began, but Jason closed the door firmly and turned to Wayne. "Hey, we've got an hour before the game starts. Let's get them tired out. Then they'll leave us alone."

"How do we do that?"

"Follow me." Jason picked Leah up and walked upstairs into the girls' bedroom. Devorah smiled at him adoringly from her crib. "She always cries when my mom leaves the house, so she put her up here with a bottle. Hey, tootsie pop, want to play?" he asked, putting Leah down and hoisting Devorah over the crib bars.

"Play Jasee, play Jasee," Leah began to chant, jumping up and down. Jason grabbed a small pillow from a crib and tossed it at Leah. She picked it up from where it had fallen and tried to throw it at Jason. The momentum made her fall forward, but when she got up, she was laughing. Wayne picked up the pillow next and threw it toward Devorah. She looked at him for a moment with large, quiet eyes, then grabbed the pillow with both hands and threw it toward his outstretched hands. It fell a foot in front of her.

"Quite an arm you have there, girl," Wayne said, snatching the pillow up. "Now watch the man do it." He wound up slowly, as if he was pitching a softball, and then tossed the pillow to the little girl. Leah pounced on it, ran over to Wayne, and pushed it against his knees.

"Okay, he's winding up, folks, he's releasing it, here it comes, and it's gone," Jason announced, sitting down on the floor, and bopping Devorah on her head and backside with another pillow, while she tried fruitlessly to grab it. He shifted it from hand to hand as his half-sister twisted and turned, giggling.

When she began to pout, he dropped the pillow and grabbed her hands, clapping them together. "How about we play hit Jasee, okay? I bet you can't hit me, I bet you can't," he coaxed, covering his head with his arms. Both Leah and Devorah immediately raced to grab the pillows and began to pummel their big brother. "This is their favorite," Jason grunted, as he rolled from side to side.

"Hit Wayne, hit Wayne." Wayne took on the same posture and grinned at the girls. Leah was the first to drop her pillow, rush over and begin to smack him, and Devorah soon joined her. "Hey, don't hit me! Use those pillows. These girls are racists!"

Jason laughed so hard he began to hiccup. "Make nice to Wayne. Don't hurt him." Devorah tentatively reached out a dimpled hand and began to stroke Wayne's cheek. "That's a good girl."

"These girls are something," Wayne said as he got up. "What do we do with them now?"

"Let's go down to the kitchen. They're always ready to eat."

The boys each took a toddler's hand and slowly made their way down the stairs. "Juice or milk?" Jason asked Leah as he leaned on the open refrigerator door.

"Juice."

"Apple or orange?"

"Apple."

"She sure knows what she wants." Wayne chuckled.

"Oh, yeah? Just watch this." Jason poured apple juice into a small plastic glass and handed it to the little girl. She grasped the glass in one hand, smilled at her brother, and then let go. Juice spilled all over as the glass bounced on the tile.

"What'd she do that for?" Wayne cried.

"Don't ask me. She does it all the time. My mother's ready to kill her. No, no, Leah, don't drop it. That's bad." Jason dropped a paper towel on the spill and pushed it around with his shoe. Then he poured some more juice in the glass.

"Juice?" Leah tried again, reaching for the glass.

"No way. I hold the cup or you don't get a drink."

Leah frowned as she tried to grab the cup from Jason. He held it out of her reach and warned her, "No. I hold the cup."

"Me hold," Leah demanded, hitting Jason's thigh with her fist.

"No, me hold."

Wayne took the cup from Jason's hand and crouched down. "Hey, let's both hold it, okay? Let's hold the cup together."

Distracted by this new offer, Leah put her hands on top of Wayne's and sipped from the cup of apple juice. When he held it out to Devorah, she did the same thing.

"Yo, you're the master, the baby master," Jason said, glancing at the clock over the sink. "Hey, the game's about to start. Let's go into the family room."

The two boys settled onto the sofa and lifted the girls to sit next to them. Jason clicked on the pregame show. Leah quickly clambered down and ran to a toy chest that stood against the wall. Pulling a large, battered picture book out, she brought it to Wayne. "Read," she instructed.

"Read? Uh, okay. 'Bert and Ernie were expecting a guest,'" he began. Devorah leaned against her brother, put her thumb in her mouth, and began to suck contentedly. Leah listened for about three minutes, then pulled the book out of Wayne's hands. Going back to the toy box, she drew out another large book.

"Read," she said, handing the next book to Wayne.

"What was wrong with Bert and Ernie, girl? Didn't you like that one?"

"She does that all the time," Jason interrupted. "Leah, go play with your blocks. Build a big tower." He grabbed the remote control and began to push buttons.

Within a minute or two, Leah was back, tugging at his hand. "Look."

"I'll look later. Go make another one." He turned to Wayne. "Do you want something to eat? I think we have a bag of chips and sodas in the kitchen."

"Yeah, I'm pretty hungry. Bring whatever you've got."

When Jason got up, Devorah, who was almost asleep, fell over and began to cry. "Oops, sorry," Jason said, propping her up, but she cried even harder. "Okay, okay, don't cry. I'm getting potato chips. You want some chips?"

Devorah's cries quieted and she began to suck her thumb again. Jason quickly left the room and returned with a big bag of chips, a box of animal crackers, and two cans of soda. "Are we ready or what? I have a good feeling about this game, Wayne. We're going to win big."

As soon as the girls saw the bag of chips, they moved toward their brother. "Gimmee chip," said Leah.

"I brought you animal crackers. See, animal crackers."

"Want chip." Leah began to pull on the bag Jason had tucked under his arm.

"Hey, cut that out!" He pushed her aside with his knee so he could get to the coffee table in front of the sofa. "You'll take what I give you. I'm in charge here. Mommy said."

"Wow, what a catch," Wayne said. "Did you see that? It was something else."

"You're kidding! I missed it because of these two pains in the neck. We have to park them somewhere so we can watch in peace. Wait, I've got an idea." Jason picked up the chip bag and waved it in front of Leah and Devorah. "How about if you eat this in the kitchen. You can color in there too. Color me a picture, a big, big picture, okay."

"'Kay," the girls agreed in unison, running into the kitchen.

"I'm going to get their coloring books and stuff and leave them in there," Jason told Wayne, following his sisters. "My mother has those little gadgets on the cabinet doors, so they can't get to the knives or nothing. Otherwise, we'll never get to watch anything."

"Okay, man, it's your house." Wayne popped a few animal crackers in his mouth and kept his eyes on the TV.

Within minutes Jason was back. "Okay, they've got crayons and markers and coloring books and some of their dolls. That should keep them busy for a long time. And we can hear if anything goes wrong. What's going on here?"

Wayne filled him in on the game so far, and the boys settled back with their sodas in their hands. The sounds of the girls drifted in every now and then, but they were happy sounds, not frightened ones, so Jason ignored them.

By the sixth inning, the Mets were up 4 to 3. Jason and Wayne were high-fiving each other when they heard the front door open and Shari call out, "Boys, we're home." Seconds later, she appeared at the family room door. "Why is it so quiet? Where are the girls?"

"They've been real good, Mom. They're coloring in the kitchen," Jason told his mother, his attention still on the game.

Suddenly they heard David's voice boom, "What the hell happened here?"

Jason jumped off the sofa and raced after his mother to the kitchen. His sisters were sitting in the middle of the floor, crushed potato chips surrounding them like sand. Pages of their coloring books, with crayon scrawls all over, were scattered about the room. Blotches of red, yellow, and blue marker were all over the linoleum tile floor. Jason could see that the girls had continued to color the floor when they'd reached the end of the paper by the sharp, neat edges the blotches of color had. Sesame Street place mats had gotten the color treatment too. Leah and Devorah had pulled them off the table and left them on the floor, along with the paper napkins and the salt and pepper shakers.

"Oh, my God, I can't believe it," Shari moaned. "How could you let them do this, Jason?"

"I didn't let them, they did it themselves. I was watching the game."

David picked up his daughters, holding one on each arm. When he stood up and turned toward Jason, his face was twisted with anger. "You were supposed to be baby-sitting, not watching the game, you stupid jerk. How could you leave them alone in the kitchen? Didn't you think about what could happen? What if they'd turned on the stove? What if something hot had fallen on them? What if they'd choked?" David was shaking with fury. "You are the most selfish, self-centered brat I ever met. All you care about is yourself. They could have been killed, and you wouldn't even have noticed. I told you, Shari, I didn't feel right about this. We're lucky there isn't blood all over the floor instead of crayon."

Frightened by the anger in David's voice, the girls began to whimper. "I'm going to clean them up," he said, staring at Jason. "I can't stand to look at you right now."

Jason felt dizzy, as if he was about to faint. "Wayne, it's time for you to go home now," his mother said, her voice low. "You can talk to Jason tomorrow."

"I'll talk to you later, man. Uh, you don't have to pay me or nothing, Mrs. Siegel," Wayne said, heading for the door. "I'm sorry the girls made a mess."

"That's all right, Wayne, this can all be cleaned up. You weren't the one responsible here, after all. That was Jason's job."

Jason looked at his mother. Did she hate him too?

Chapter 10

Jason kneeled in front of his bed and spread a relatively new stack of cards out in front of him. Looking at the gleaming photographs always soothed him, and now he peered closely at a hologram of one of his favorite players, trying to forget what had happened. The glittering figure seemed to move when he shifted the card slightly.

Dinner had been quiet and tense. Leah and Devorah had smiled and chattered as usual, but David hadn't said a word to Jason, and his mother hadn't cracked a joke either. It had taken Jason and his mother over an hour to clean up the mess in the kitchen. When he'd tried to explain that it wasn't really his fault, Shari had told him grimly that she didn't want to hear his excuses and he should keep scrubbing.

Jason heard a knock. "Yeah?" He reached out to turn down his radio.

David opened the door. "Hi. What are you doing?"

"Nothing much." Jason clenched his jaw, getting ready for something, though he wasn't sure what.

David took a few steps forward and then stopped. "Jason, you know I was very upset by what happened today."

"Yeah, but how was I supposed to know they couldn't be alone?" Jason began his defense. "You should have told me—"

"I think you should have known," David interrupted, "but that's not what I came to say. I came to apologize."

"To apologize? To me?"

"I shouldn't have spoken to you that way. I'm sorry. It's wrong to insult people."

Jason looked at David with deep suspicion. What was he talking about? "The Talmud tells us that insulting someone or calling them names is like killing them," David went on. "So I owe you an apology," he repeated.

Jason stared at his stepfather, momentarily speechless. "You mean I'm not grounded or anything?"

David looked back at him. "No, you're not grounded," he said quietly. "I hope you realize the danger Leah and Devorah could have been in. They're just babies, Jason. We have to take care of them. They can't do it for themselves."

Jason flushed and turned back to his cards. "I know. It was pretty dumb."

"Yes, it was."

Jason heard David turn around and head toward the door. "I'm sorry," he murmured to his cards.

By Tuesday, things were back to normal. David and Jason were talking to each other again, and Shari was absorbed in running after the twins and keeping up with the laundry. Only a faint blue patch remained on one floor tile. When Wayne reminded him that they had a game on Saturday at the end of the week, Jason had almost forgotten about the previous Sunday.

"Are you going to come over to my house to change the way you did last time?"

"I don't know," Jason said, moving along the lunch line. His mother had packed him a tuna salad sandwich. He could have milk with that, he figured quickly. Picking up the container, he turned to Wayne. "I haven't thought about it. I guess so. It worked the last time." He couldn't use his grandfather again, though.

Jason waited as Wayne opened his lunch bag. Mrs. Duggins always packed enough food for three people, it seemed. He watched as Wayne spread out a ham-and-cheese sandwich on a hero roll, a bag of taco chips, an apple, a banana, and a small candy bar.

Wayne studied his sandwich. "Man, she knows I don't like mustard. What do you have?"

"Tuna."

"I like tuna. Want to trade?"

Jason hesitated. "No, I can't. Yours isn't kosher."

"Oh, yeah. Mixing meat and dairy is a no-no, too, right?"

"Yes-yes."

The boys chewed silently until Mike blew a straw wrapper at Wayne. Then Jason balled up a bit of bread and tossed it back, the girls at the table began to scream, and everyone got into the lunchroom mood.

"I need another excuse," Jason explained as he and Wayne walked home from school. "My grandfather warned me not to use him again."

"So, where are you allowed to go?"

"Nowhere, that's what stinks. No movies, no mall, no card shows, no fun. The only thing I can do is visit and sleep."

"So tell your folks you're taking a long nap, about five hours long."

"Right, and when my mom comes to see if I'm still alive, she'll think I've been kidnapped."

"No good."

"No good," Jason agreed. "Wait a minute. There's some kids' program run by my synagogue this Saturday. The Hebrew school teachers have been telling us about it for weeks. We're all supposed to meet at Veterans Park in the middle of town and talk about helping the homeless or something. What if I tell them I'm going to that?"

"Will they believe it?"

"I don't know. I've never gone to any others. They're a bunch of nerds. But maybe I can convince my mom I'm so bored I'll do anything to get out of the house."

"Go for it. It's the best we've come up with."

Jason nodded, wondering silently how much longer he could keep this up. Then he thought of Corsello and the unfairness of it all. "That's what I'll tell them."

"Of course you can go," Shari said when Jason mentioned that he wanted to attend the synagogue youth group's get-together in the park. She was so pleased, it was pathetic, Jason thought. "What are they doing there?" she asked, checking her recipe for vegetarian lasagna.

"I don't know exactly," Jason answered. "Jewish stuff," he couldn't help adding, as he crammed a cream-filled cupcake into his mouth.

It took a moment for Shari to respond. She gave him a sideways glance, then asked. "Do you think you could tell David at dinner without being snotty? It would mean a lot to him."

Jason was silent. Could he tell another lie? He had already told so many. "Yeah, sure," he murmured, then walked away.

Saturday morning services seemed to go much faster than usual that week, and Jason was surprised to find Shabbat lunch over and Shari and David ready to head upstairs for their nap before he knew it. He'd have to start acting now.

"So, when are you leaving, Jase?" his mother asked as she puttered aimlessly around the kitchen.

"Pretty soon, I guess. We're supposed to be at the park at two-thirty."

"And when is it over? Do you need to be picked up somewhere?"

"No, no. I think we're going back to the synagogue after for something to eat. I can always get a ride home with someone. You don't have to do anything."

"Okay," his mother said, patting his cheek. "Have a good time. I know it can get a little boring around here on Saturdays, so I'm glad this came up."

"Right. So, I'll see you later, I guess."

His mother folded the meat dish towel and left the room. Jason stared at his black dress shoes for a while, then slowly climbed the stairs to his room. He changed out of his Shabbat clothes into sweatpants and a T-shirt, grabbed his Mets warm-up jacket, and slipped out the front door.

When he got to Wayne's house, his stomach hurt as if a fist was squeezing his guts. "Hey, man, change your clothes before my mom sees you. I told her we were walking to the field together."

"What's she doing home?" Jason hissed.

"She said she just needed a day off. My dad didn't have a lot of patients today. Hurry!"

Jason ran up the stairs to Wayne's room, fear making his heart pound. He was always afraid lately, it seemed. As he struggled to catch his breath, he felt as if his legs weighed a thousand pounds each. He was so tired, he wished he were at home taking a nap, too.

Wayne stuck his head in the door. "Are you ready yet? What are you staring at? You look like some UFO has taken over your body."

Jason began to twitch. "They stuck wires in me. They made me do horrible things. That's why I'm going to have an alien baby!" he moaned. He slammed his Ace cap on his head. "I guess I'm ready. Let's go."

A smiling Mrs. Duggins was waiting at the foot of the stairs when they came down. "I hope your arm feels fine, Jason. I hear you're playing a tough team. Daddy and I will go over a little later, Wayne. We're looking forward to watching the game. Good luck, now."

"Thanks, Mrs. Duggins."

Wayne kissed his mother good-bye, and the boys walked out onto the street. "Walk me down to Veterans Park. I'll hang around for a while, then I'll meet you at the field. I told my mom I was going to this thing, so I should show up at least," Jason said.

Wayne looked at him quizzically. "You mean you don't want to tell a whole lie, just a little part of one?"

Jason pulled his cap lower over his eyes. "Let's just go. It's not out of your way."

The magnolias were blooming in Veterans Park, and the weedy lawn was pocked with crushed pink-satin blossoms. A large group of boys and girls—more girls than boys, Jason noted—were gathered around the bandstand. They looked at him curiously as he got closer. "Hey, Jase, what are you dressed up for? This isn't a costume party," one of the boys in his Hebrew school class called out.

Jason realized instantly he had made a mistake. Coming here in his uniform was stupid. Everyone would know he was going to a game. Whenever anyone showed up at Hebrew school in uniform, it meant they were leaving early to play ball.

Jason turned and began to jog away. What was he going to do now? What if someone called his mother? What if one of the teachers had seen him?

As soon as he was out of sight of the park, Jason slowed down. He tried to get his mind to think clearly, but he could feel panic begin to choke him. There was nothing he could do to fix things now, he told himself. If someone had seen him and wanted to call his house, he couldn't stop them. Of course, no one was answering the phone at his house, not until tonight, anyway.

Jason got to the field in time to warm up with the team. "Okay, Siegel, get out there with Duggins and catch some flies," Corsello barked when he saw him. "Let's get ready. We got a game to play."

Chapter 11

"Siegel, you're up after Lindenbaum." Jason dropped his cap and mitt, pulled on his batter's glove, and walked over to the batter's box. The stands were full, as they were for all the weekend games, and the warm spring sunshine seemed to have drawn even more people than usual. Dr. and Mrs. Duggins were just settling themselves on the highest bleacher, Jason noticed, and Mike's dad was there too. Mrs. Appelbaum had staked out her usual seat right at the beginning of the game.

By the end of the second inning, the score was tied 2–2, and Corsello had made it clear that he expected some runs in the upcoming inning. Jason swung hard in the on-deck circle, hoping to get some of the tension out of his shoulders and his mind on the game.

Mike had two strikes and two balls when the pitcher lobbed one right across the plate. It was a clean hit down center field, and Mike was dancing on second base as Jason came up to bat. He adjusted his helmet, choked up a little like Grandpa Phil always told him to do, and looked out at the mound. The first pitch was way outside, and he didn't bother to swing. "Ball," the umpire called, sounding bored. The second pitch looked good, just a little low, and Jason kept his eye on the ball as his bat reached out to meet it. It felt like a single, and sure enough, he was safe on first when the second baseman grabbed the ball.

Kevin Hogan was up next. Jason spread his legs out wide and moved in the direction of second, watching for the chance to steal. It came when the catcher bobbled. It was just a few seconds, but it was enough.

Jason heard the other team's coach begin to scream as soon as he started running. "Throw to second! Throw to second!" Holding his hands out stiffly in front, Jason threw himself toward the base. Dirt flew up his nose and into his open mouth, and a searing pain shot through his forearm as his left hand snapped back against the baseman's foot. Jason had never felt such pain. It was as if his hand had suddenly caught fire. His shriek coincided with the umpire's call, "He's out!"

"What do you mean, he's out!" Corsello bellowed, running toward them. "He touched the bag. Didn't you, Siegel?" Jason was cradling his left hand against his chest and desperately trying not to cry. "Hey, what's the matter with you? Are you hurt?"

"I must have twisted my hand or something. It'll be all right." Jason got to his knees slowly, and then shakily stood up, still shielding his hand. The

burning pain had changed to a persistent throbbing. "Maybe I should put some ice on it or something."

Corsello and the umpire both looked at Jason's hand. When the coach tried to brush the dirt away, Jason gasped and tears sprung to his eyes. "Come on back to the bench; you're out anyway," Corsello said. "I've got an ice pack there."

Jason walked across the field to Ace's bench, Corsello's arm around his shoulder. He felt suddenly cold, even though the sun was still shining brightly. His left wrist was beginning to swell now, and the skin was turning purple. "Sit down here, Jason, and keep this on your wrist." Corsello wrapped a blue plastic bag filled with something ice-cold around Jason's hand. The cold hurt just as much as the throbbing. "Are your folks here?"

"My folks? Uh, no, they're not here."

"Are they at home? I'm going to call them. Maybe they should take you to the hospital."

"No, no, don't call them. I'm okay. The ice bag is helping. It already doesn't hurt so much. I'll just sit here for a while until I feel better, okay?"

Corsello look at him doubtfully for a second, then turned back to the game. The pain in Jason's wrist seemed to fill his whole arm and was moving toward his shoulder. What if his hand was broken? What would he tell his mother when he got home? Maybe he could say he'd fallen.

"Well, Jason, what happened to you?" a deep voice asked.

Jason turned around slowly. Dr. Duggins was standing on the other side of the dugout. "I guess I twisted my wrist. The coach put ice on it."

"Come over here. Let me take a look."

Jason's head spun as he slowly stood up and walked toward Wayne's father. He lifted the ice pack and waited as Dr. Duggins peered at his hand. "Hmm, that doesn't look too good. I bet it hurts, doesn't it?"

Jason nodded weakly, then replaced the ice pack. "It'll get better soon. The coach can relieve me for the next inning." Jason turned and went back to the bench before Dr. Duggins could say any more. He felt an overwhelming desire to lay down and sleep. He wished his mom were there.

In a few minutes, Dr. Duggins was back. "I called your house, Jason, but no one answered the phone. Did your parents go somewhere?"

"I don't know. They usually take naps on Saturday afternoons, and they don't talk on the phone."

Dr. Duggins looked puzzled. "Well, I left a message. Anyway, I'll give you a ride home if you need one."

Jason felt too tired to say thanks. He turned back to the game and tried to ignore the pain rolling up his arm. The figures on the field looked blurry, and he couldn't figure out what was happening. Was that Wayne on third base? Where was Mike, then?

Jason blinked, but his vision did not become clearer. Maybe he was going blind. He suddenly remembered the hospital bed his father slept in when he was really sick. Jason was frightened of hospitals and hoped he wouldn't have to go. How would he get there, anyway?

"Jason, what happened to you? Are you all right?" Michelle stood in front of him and looked down at his swollen hand. "That looks really gross. It's all purple. Do you want my mother to call your house or something?"

"No, nobody needs to call my house. They won't answer the phone anyway."

"Well, I have to go. Coach Corsello told the kids to leave you alone; that's why they're sitting at the other end."

Jason blearily watched Michelle walk over and put on a helmet. He was suddenly terribly thirsty. He was thinking of asking one of the kids to buy him a drink at the snack bar when he heard someone calling his name. "Jason! Jason!"

Jason turned to look in the direction of the voice. It sounded familiar, but different. David was running toward him from the parking lot, dressed in sweats. His hair wasn't combed, and he was wearing flip-flops. He raced around the front of the dugout, panting. "What happened? Was there an accident?" When he saw the swollen hand, he gasped. "Oh, my God! Come on, we have to go to the hospital."

David pulled Jason up gently and positioned himself so the injured hand was next to his own body. Leading him over to Corsello, he said, "I'm taking him to the emergency room for an X-ray, Coach."

"Yeah, that makes sense. The only reason I didn't call you was Jason told me you weren't around. I would have brought him home right after the game."

"That's okay. Dr. Duggins left a message on the answering machine, so I came right over." David began to turn Jason toward the parking lot. "We better get over there right away. This looks bad."

"Yeah, yeah," Corsello agreed. "Let me know how he is. Take it easy, Jason."

Jason stumbled along next to David and carefully climbed into the van's front seat. He wished his mother had come for him instead, but she had probably stayed home to watch the twins. His stepfather closed the door behind him and came around to the driver's side. Leaning over Jason, he pulled out the seat belt. "Just lift that hand, and I'll buckle this for you." Jason silently did as he was told. "We couldn't believe it when we heard Dr. Duggins leave his message. Mommy said you were at a youth group event. I guess you got bored at the synagogue and decided to go over to the game?" David's voice didn't sound angry, so Jason ventured to look over. "What I can't figure out, though, is whose uniform you're wearing."

If Jason hadn't felt so wretched, he would have been embarrassed. As it was, he smiled weakly and kept quiet. He didn't feel like getting into an argument.

David turned the ignition key and backed out of the space. Shifting into drive, he sped out of the lot and onto the potholed street. He looked over when Jason instinctively flinched. "Sorry. I'll slow down. It'll take a little longer to get there, but you'll be more comfortable."

"That's okay. I'm all right. I didn't expect to leave until the end of the game anyway. You didn't have to come."

"Why is that? That's probably broken, you know."

"I knew you wouldn't drive because it's Shabbat and all. I told them not to call you, that you wouldn't answer the phone."

David didn't say anything, and when Jason looked over at him, his face was dark with anger. "You thought I wouldn't take you to the hospital to fix a broken wrist? You must think I'm a real son of a bitch." David slowly made a left turn onto the street that led to Shady Glen Community Hospital. "You think I'd let you sit there because it's Shabbat? What if Leah fell down the stairs and split her skull open? You think I'd wait until Saturday night? What if Mommy got sick? You think I'd wait until Sunday to help her? What kind of jerk do you think I am?" David's voice dropped, and he sounded tired. "Jason, I don't know how to get through to you. If you think I'd do that, you don't know me at all."

Jason was too shocked to answer for a moment; then words began to spill out of his mouth. "How am I supposed to know what you will do and what you won't? You're always coming up with new rules. I can't even remember them all. I can't do this, and I can't do that. And you never ask me if I want to; it's just this is the way it's going to be. We never worried about this stuff before you showed up. You think you can change everything, but you can't. You can't just show up and make everything different. You're not my father. My father's dead!" Jason heard his voice become a squeal. His heart was pounding, and it was hard to talk over the lump in his throat. He took a deep breath. "It's just that you're so religious, and I know you're not allowed to drive on Shabbat unless it's life and death or something, and I'm not going to die from a broken wrist…." Jason stopped talking and stared at the dashboard.

David drove in silence for a while. Then he said quietly, "I know I'm not your real father, Jason, but you're my real son. Does that make sense?"

Jason shook his head. He was afraid to take his eyes off the dashboard.

"I knew your father. We went to school together. He was a great guy, and I can never take his place. But you're the only son I have, so you don't have to take anyone's place. You don't have to stop loving your father for me to love you."

Jason began to feel light-headed. "I guess I was scared that you'd be mad at me for playing, too."

"I am mad at you, and disappointed that you've been lying to us all this time, but I still wouldn't let you suffer, Shabbat or not. Following the rules in the Torah is not a substitute for doing the right thing. It's a guide to help people know what the right thing to do is. You'll see"—David glanced at him—"or maybe you do already, that knowing what's right can be very hard. Sometimes there's more than one way to be right, or a lot of different ways to be wrong, and you have to pick among them. Keeping Shabbat is important to me, but it's not as important as taking care of my family, of the people I love, like you. I'd break any rule to do that."

Jason felt as if he were choking. Suddenly, huge sobs burst out of him. "Oh, it hurts so bad." He was gasping for breath. "I was so scared. I didn't know what to do." It was as if some alien force had taken over his body. All he could do was cry and cry.

When David pulled into the emergency-room parking lot, Jason's sobs had slowed down, and he was hiccuping and trying to stop his nose from running with his good arm. "Come on down," David said softly, opening the passenger door. "Let's go inside and check in. Then we'll call Mommy. She's probably frantic by now."

Jason shuffled into the hospital and sat down in one of a row of connected blue plastic chairs. He watched David go up to the nurse at the desk and show her something in his wallet. Then he stood for a while longer while the nurse wrote stuff down. Jason looked about him. A woman with a baby on her lap sat across from him and smiled when his eyes met hers. A few seats down was a young man wearing jeans and a muscle T-shirt. He had a huge bandage wrapped around his arm. Jason could see blood seeping through. The only other people waiting were a fat lady and an old, old man.

"Okay, son, we shouldn't have to wait too long, the nurse said. She's going to call Dr. Michaels, the orthopedist who set Mommy's ankle a few years ago. We'll be home in an hour maybe." Jason recalled his mother hobbling around on crutches after she'd twisted her ankle jogging. That was before the twins were born. "They're going to take an X-ray first, and we're supposed to wait here until they call us. How about a soda while we're waiting?"

Jason nodded, and David went over to a vending machine. In a minute, he was back with two sodas and a bag of cheese puffs. Jason studied the bag before he opened it. "It doesn't have that little sign that means it's kosher."

"You can make an exception today, I guess."

Jason set the bag aside and took the open soda can David held out to him. "I'm not hungry, anyway. I just want a drink."

David sat down next to him and began to sip his own soda. "I called Mom and told her what happened."

Jason took a long drink. The sweet, cold soda felt good going down. "How come you like being religious so much?" he asked suddenly. "Don't you get mad at all the stuff you can't do?"

"You mean like eat bacon cheeseburgers or watch TV on Saturday?" At Jason's nod, he continued, "Well, it took me a while to get used to it, but now I don't miss it at all. You know how Mommy teases that I was always a do-gooder? It's true. I always liked being part of something, and I always wanted to be a good person. That's why I've always been on committees to do this or the other, I guess. But it's not easy to do the right thing; it's not easy to know what the right thing is." David stopped talking and took a long drink. When he spoke again, his voice was husky. "Marrying your mother was the right thing. She gave me the family I've always wanted, and you're part of that, Jason. All of you—Leah, Devorah, you, and Mommy—are the most important things in the world to me. There's nothing I wouldn't do for you. I should have talked to you about keeping kosher and observing Shabbat; you're right about that. It was wrong to just spring it on you, but it seemed so natural and great to me, I wanted to share it."

Jason finished his soda. "I guess I can live without pepperoni pizza, but I really hate hanging around the house all day Saturday, especially during baseball season. Playing baseball isn't work, and it's not like shopping. It's just a game, and I don't see why I can't play."

David laughed, stretched his legs out, and put his arm around the back of Jason's chair. "You sound like you're making a rabbinical argument. The

Talmud is full of dissenting opinions, you know, on every question. Well, the rest of this season is out, buddy, but we'll talk about next year when we get home."

A woman in a blue uniform walked over to them, studying a clipboard in her hand. "Are you David Siegel?" she asked Jason.

Jason looked over at David. "No, no, that's my dad," he said. "My name's Jason."

OTHER TITLES FROM ALEF DESIGN GROUP & TORAH AURA PRODUCTIONS

MIDDLE READERS—8-11 YEARS OLD

NEW! *Gabriel's Ark* by *Sandra R. Curtis*

Gabriel's Ark is a touching book about a family's dedication to passing on their Jewish heritage to Gabriel, their disabled son. As preparations for Gabriel's bar mitzvah begin, readers learn how each family member has his/her own role in nurturing Gabriel through this important ritual event. Throughout the story the rainbow and Noah's ark become powerful symbols for Gabriel's inclusion in the Jewish community.

$7.95 • 1-881283-22-4 • SOFTCOVER • JEWISH LIFE, SPECIAL NEEDS, BAR MITZVAH

NEW! *The Saturday Secret* by *Miriam Rinn*

Jason Siegel thinks his stepfather's religious observances have gone far enough. First only kosher food at home. Then he is forced to wear a kippah. Now no baseball games on Shabbat! Jason is determined to play baseball—no matter what. But when his plan backfires, Jason finds himself entangled in a situation that hurts his teammate's feelings and jeopardizes his relationship with his mother and step-father.

$7.95 • 1-881283-26-7 • SOFTCOVER• SELF-DISCOVERY, JUDAISM

The Grey Striped Shirt by Jacqueline Jules

 Frannie is looking for Grandma's purple hat with the feather. By accident she discovers a grey striped shirt with a yellow star hidden in the back of the closet. As she begins asking her grandparents questions, they begin to unfold the story of their Holocaust experience. This novel for middle readers gently reveals the truths about the Holocaust without reducing it to a horror show.

$8.50 • ISBN #1-881283-21-6 • Softcover • Holocaust

Dear Hope... Love, Grandma by Hilda A. Hurwitz & Hope R. Wasburn, Edited by Mara H. Wasburn

 Eight-year-old Hope had a school project to become the summer pen pal of a senior citizen. When her assigned pen pal failed to write back, her mother suggested she write to her grandmother. A two-year correspondence resulted. This book is a collection of letters in which Grandma reveals the stories of her childhood, the difficulties growing up in turn-of-the-century St. Louis, and some wonderful and joyous insights about human hearts.

$13.95 • ISBN #1-881283-03-8 • Hardcover • Autobiography

Two Cents & a Milk Bottle by Lee Batterman

 This outstanding juvenile novel, set in 1937, follows twelve-year-old Leely Dorman as she faces a new neighborhood, a new school and new friends. Over the course of the novel, Leely becomes a friend, an entrepreneur, and the first girl in the neighborhood to study to become a bat mitzvah. A wonderful ending ties in themes of the Hanukkah holiday.

$15.95 • 1-881283-17-8 • Hardcover • American Jewish History

Sing Time *by Bruce H. Siegel*

A ten-year-old discovers in half an hour how a single teacher, a Cantor, can impact his life. This Cantor doesn't just sing songs, he shares the value of a single moment in time, and how music is the "calendar" of Jewish life. Cantor Jacobs steers our hero down a path he might never have taken otherwise, all because his dad decided that Jerry-the-Jerk (his older brother, Gerald) should have a bar mitzvah.

$5.95 • ISBN # 1-881283-14-3 • SOFTCOVER • JEWISH CONNECTIONS

Tanta Teva & the Magic Booth
by Joel Lurie Grishaver

It all started when Marc (with a "C") Zeiger ran away one night to get his parents to buy him a Virtual Reality hookup (it's a long story). In the dark, lost in a part of the woods which couldn't possibly exist, he encounters Tanta Teva, a cleaning lady who is busy scrubbing graffiti off rocks in the forest. Together they visit young Joshua, David and Hillel. When Marc returns home, no one really believes the stories of where he'd been and who he'd met!

$5.95 • ISBN #1-881283-00-3 • SOFTCOVER • MIDDLE READER • FANTASY

The Passover Passage *by Susan Atlas*

Rebecca Able is having a most memorable Passover. She is sailing in the Caribbean with her grandparents aboard their sailboat, the Diaspora. On this unforgettable trip, Becca learns not only how a Passover Seder is celebrated on board a sailboat, but also about freedom, opportunity, family, and Judaism. A real adventure.

$5.95 • ISBN #0-933873-46-8 • SOFTCOVER • JEWISH LIFE, PASSOVER

Sofer: The Story of a Torah Scroll
by Dr. Eric Ray

Writing a Torah is a labor of love that requires patience, knowledge and skill. Eric Ray is a gentle, wise man, a skilled artist, and a learned Jew. In this read-aloud text and color photo essay, Eric shares both his craft and his passion.

$6.95 • 0-933873-98-0 • SOFTCOVER • TORAH SCROLL, SCRIBES, CALLIGRAPHY

YOUNG ADULT—11-14 YEARS OLD

NEW! *Keeping Faith in the Dust* by Fran Maltz

This is a unique recounting of a familiar story—the siege of Masada in the first century C.E.—from the diary of a teenage girl. Hannah begins her journal as a young girl of thirteen. As Hannah's family is forced to move first to Jerusalem, and then to Masada, her religious awakening provides her with the strength and inspiration to endure persecution, terror and shattering personal loss.

$7.95 • 1-881283-25-9 • SOFTCOVER • YOUNG ADULT • JEWISH HISTORY

Champion & Jewboy by Bruce M. Siegel

Champion & Jewboy are two novellas dealing with anti-Semitism. In *Champion*, a sixteen-year-old digs into his grandfather's hidden past. *Jewboy* features a teenager convicted of vandalizing a synagogue who is transported back through time to witness, and become a participant in, a number of the most famous anti-Semitic events of the twentieth century.

$6.95 • ISBN #1-883123-11-9 • SOFTCOVER • ANTI-SEMITISM, NAZI GERMANY

Bar Mitzvah Lessons *by Martin Elsant*

David Silverberg is the worst bar mitzvah student in all of recorded Jewish history. No one can teach him until his father takes him to Rabbi Reuven Weiss, a mechanic and a rebel. This novel is the story of how they change each other's lives and how David grows to become a bar mitzvah.

$5.95 • ISBN #1-883123-01-1 • SOFTCOVER • BAR MITZVAH

The Swastika on the Synagogue Door *by J. Leonard Romm*

When a suburban synagogue on Long Island is attacked by anti-Semitic vandals, the hatred manifest in the spray paint forces the Lazarus kids to confront their own history, their own prejudice, and find the guilty party.

$6.95 • ISBN #1-881283-05-4 • SOFTCOVER • ANTI-SEMITISM

PICTURE BOOKS

A Sense of Shabbat *by Faige Kobre*

A Sense of Shabbat

Faige Kobre

Torah Aura Productions

In the sensuous photographs and simple text that make up this picture book, the taste, feel, sound, look and touch of the Jewish Sabbath all come alive. The Sabbath presented here is at once holy and wondrous, comfortable and familiar.

$11.95 • ISBN #0-933873-44-1 • HARDCOVER • SABBATH

Eight Nights, Eight Lights

by Rabbi Kerry M. Olitzky

Courage. Gratitude. Sharing. Knowledge. Service. Understanding. Love. Hope. Eight nights. Eight lights. Eight family values. In this joyous and reflective work, Rabbi Kerry M. Olitzky provides families with a way of letting their Hanukkah celebrations affirm not only their Jewish identity, but the very Jewish values they wish to transmit to their children.

$8.95 • ISBN #1-881283-09-7 • SOFTCOVER • FAMILY/HANUKKAH

Mark Stark's Amazing Jewish Cookbook

This cookbook is a collection of secret family recipes and a celebration of Jewish cooking. Everything is ready for even the most beginning cook—hand-drawn recipes show the ingredients, the tools needed, and the steps used to make them. Recipes are listed by holiday, with a description of the holiday's celebration. All recipes are coded for adherence to kashrut, the religious and dietary laws of the Jewish people. For those who want to discover the fun of creative Jewish cooking, this book is a must.

$26.50 • ISBN #1-881283-19-4 • SOFTCOVER • COOKING/JEWISH LIFE